The Apache Attacked!

Clint yanked his rifle out of its scabbard. He levered a shell into the chamber and hurried back to join Earl. They were going to make a stand that these Apache would never forget. And even if they lost, the price would be very, very costly.

Clint dropped down onto one knee and sighted in on the first Indian. He took a deep breath and squeezed the trigger and the man lifted off his pony as if pulled by an invisible wire.

"Nice shooting," Earl grunted. "And if we just had us a cannon or a Gatling gun, maybe we'd get outta this alive!"

Don't miss any of the lusty, hard-riding action
in the Charter Western series, THE GUNSMITH

And coming next month:
THE GUNSMITH #61: THE COMSTOCK GOLD FRAUD

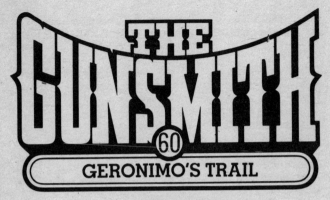

THE GUNSMITH

60

GERONIMO'S TRAIL

J. R. ROBERTS

CHARTER BOOKS, NEW YORK

THE GUNSMITH #60: GERONIMO'S TRAIL

A Charter Book / published by arrangement with
the author

PRINTING HISTORY
Charter edition / December 1986

ISBN: 0-441-30964-X

Charter Books are published by The Berkley Publishing Group,
200 Madison Avenue, New York, New York 10016.
PRINTED IN THE UNITED STATES OF AMERICA

ONE

The Gunsmith just did not understand why his old friend, Ed Brisco, had settled in southeastern Arizona to play out the final days of his illustrious law career. Ed sure had enough reputation to get about any frontier sheriff's job he wanted. But he'd chosen Broken Lance, Arizona. Clint admired Arizona just fine, yet there were parts of it best suited for raising cactus, lizards, gila monsters, scorpions, rattlesnakes and Apache—in about that order of desirability. To Clint's way of thinking, anything within a hundred miles of the Mexican border was bad news. Hotter than hell and dry as the inside of a rock.

He had been passing through Tucson heading for high country when he ran into Pecos James. Pecos had once been Clint's deputy and each had saved the other from ambush once or twice.

"You heard about old Ed Brisco?" Pecos James had drawled after allowing the Gunsmith to buy the first mug of beer.

Clint had lost track of Ed's whereabouts years ago and shook his head.

"He's in Broken Lance."

"Never heard of the place."

1

"You will. There's rumors that they struck gold down there."

The Gunsmith sipped his beer. The temperature outside was nudging one hundred degrees. It was definitely time to leave these parts for a cooler territory. "That right?"

"Yep. Old Ed got hisself shot real bad sometime in the last couple of weeks."

Clint frowned. He owed Ed a few favors—like his life. "Who did it?"

"Beats me. Backshot, though."

Clint's fist tightened on the handle of his mug. "He going to live?"

"I don't know. Broken Arrow is only about a hundred miles southeast of here. Why don't you go find out?"

The Gunsmith looked closely at Pecos. He greatly respected the man's ability with a gun, but Pecos wasn't the kind to go out of his way for anybody, not even his mother. "You sure old Ed didn't just get drunk and manage to shoot himself in the leg or something? He must be seventy years old by now."

"At least," Pecos agreed. "He was older than God hisself when we worked with him. But he was backshot all right. Stagecoach driver comes in every week from them parts said there's big trouble down around Broken Lance."

"There most generally is when they have a new strike."

"It's more'n that," Pecos argued with that bulldog stubbornness that the years would never change. "Some kind of range war or somethin'."

"You want to ride down there with me and find out?"

"Nope." Pecos rolled his bloodshot eyes. "Got a hot

woman and a hot hand with the cards lately. Tucson is treatin' me right this time, Clint. You know I always did stay with what was going good."

Clint tossed back his beer. "Yeah," he said. "Besides, at this time of the year a hundred miles of Sonoran Desert is a misery."

Pecos called for two more beers. "You stay, you can room with me and my girlfriend."

"Now why would I do a thing like that?"

"You take one look at her body, you'll damn sure want her to be your girlfriend too! Five dollars a day—if she'll let us split the cost. You take her midnight to noon, she's mine from noon to midnight."

Clint shook his head with disgust. "I never pay for what I can have for free—and I don't share women."

"Shit," Pecos said with a slow grin. "You're still the ladies' man, ain't you."

"Nope, but now and then some gal will take pity on my ugliness and shower me with her kindness."

Pecos' laugh came from way down in his chest. It sounded almost like a braying mule. Clint had forgotten how much the man's laugh grated on him.

"So long, Pecos," he said.

"Wait, what about your beer! Here it comes and I'm payin' for it!"

"Drink it yourself," Clint said. "I'd rather have it when I get back."

"You go down to Broken Lance," Pecos called to the only man he knew was faster than himself, "you may never come back!"

Clint heard the warning but he did not respond. He just went to the livery, paid up his board bill and saddled Duke. It was three in the afternoon when he rode out of Tucson. Hottest time of the day and one when only a fool would go for a ride across a hundred miles of blistering desert. But Clint was a fool when it came to helping an old friend.

Fact of the matter was, Clint just did not understand a fella like Pecos James. How could that man learn about someone like Ed Brisco getting ambushed and do nothing about it? Maybe Ed needed help. Maybe he was dying and needed a friendly face. Hell, even if he was already dead he might just need someone to make sure he had a proper tombsone. One made out of marble, engraved with his name in the rock so it would last for at least as many years as the man himself had lasted. Poor men got laid under in a blanket or a pine box, and if they had any grave marker at all, it would be nothing but a pair of crossed sticks with a name crudely carved into it. Two summers later, in this country, the cross would be splintered and the name illegible. Ed Brisco deserved a whole lot more than that.

Clint had seen a lot of death and dying, but that hadn't made him indifferent to a friend in time of need. Pecos James was fearless and fast—but sometimes with a man like him, you had to wonder what his friendship really meant.

Now, as he took a shortcut trail that looped south of Tombstone and cut through the heart of the Chiricahua Apache country, Clint's every nerve and instinct for survival was finely tuned. A lot of the Apache had been killed or chased deep into Mexico, but there were still a whole lot more who raided north of the border. To Clint's way of thinking, the huge San Carlos Apache Reservation was nothing more than a staging ground for raids.

Cochise was dead now, but there was one even worse who was taking his place. An Apache named Geronimo. He was said to be as cunning as Cochise, and even more full of hate.

Whenever the word Apache was used, it just sort of put a man's neck hairs on alert. The word itself had been derived from the Navajo "apachu" meaning enemy. Apache were everyone's enemy. They showed no favorites when it came to robbing and killing. They murdered and raped whites, Mexicans and Indians from other tribes. No one was their equal and any man who thought he could outfight, outsneak or outrun them in their own backyard was a fool. From infancy, the Apache children were trained to endure pain and hardship as an everyday part of life. By the time a brave was in his teens, he could dogtrot seventy miles at a stretch doing nothing but sucking on a round pebble. That meant he could run most men on horseback to death over the long haul, across rough terrain.

Most American Indians liked beadwork. Bright eagle feather headdresses and fancy silver work, blankets or such. Not the Apache. He was as plain as this desert land. He just survived and killed whatever was edible. A Plains Indian loved his horse. Treasured a good buffalo pony above everything—even his squaw. Not the Apache. The Apache ran his poor horse until it could go no farther, then he ate the dead critter. Some gratitude for an animal that had given you its last ounce of strength!

No siree. Clint had no use for Apache. He just feared and respected them like everyone else and he sure wished he could see Broken Lance and escape the chance of coming across Apache.

He had ridden all night, his path illuminated by the moon and directed by the stars. As usual, he used the North Star as his guide. By keeping it just over his right shoulder, he guessed he'd held a pretty fair line toward his destination.

Now, it was coming dawn and he reckoned he still

had another thirty or forty miles to ride. Clint halted Duke and stepped down from the saddle. He carried two canteens, one for his horse and one for himself, though the horse got a fair share of his too.

"Ain't this country a pistol, though?" he asked Duke, pouring water into his Stetson for the animal to drink. Duke sucked up the water eagerly. And though it was only sunrise, the temperature was at least eighty and soon it would be climbing again.

Clint watched the sunrise, a big, brassy ball lifting off the eastern horizon. As soon as its roundness separated from the gentle curve of the earth, it seemed to change colors. To grow mean, angry and white-hot. "Well," Clint said feeling a little subdued by the desolate land that stretched out all around him. "We could have played it safe and followed the stage road into Tombstone. But that added another thirty miles and that's a distance in this kind of country. But maybe I should have done 'er anyway. You want to see if we can find a little shade somewheres and hole up for the day? Or would you rather just bite the bit and carry me on to Broken Lance in the heat?"

Duke seemed fresh despite the hard night and the strength-sapping, 24-hour-a-day heat. He bobbed his head up and down and used his huge tongue to lap the wet inside of Clint's hat.

"I guess that means that you want to push on, huh?"

The big gelding neighed softly.

"All right," Clint said. He capped the canteen, jammed the toe of his boot into the stirrup and mounted easily. Just slightly above average height and in his thirties Clint was slender but very strong and supple. Big-muscled men lacked his quickness and vital hand speed. Small men usually lacked his easy-going disposition and patience. Clint knew by hard experience that, in the

West, impatient men or those who lost their tempers in a fight usually lost their battles, or their lives.

Clint urged his gelding forward saying, "Just don't start complaining of the heat in a couple of hours when it starts to fry our brains."

By eight o'clock, both he and Duke were wringing wet, but by eight-thirty, he'd forgotten about the heat. He could see a thin stream of smoke lifting off the desert floor just a couple of miles ahead. White man, Mexican or Apache? Clint sure hoped it wasn't the latter. He supposed he could ride an extra ten miles and take a big loop around, but then, in this bad land with deep arroyos and brush-filled barrancas, ten miles might consume many hours. And every hour out here alone increased the danger.

Clint whipped his hat off and wiped his brow with his dirty sleeve. "That smoke is right between us and Broken Lance," he said. "I'll just have to take the chance it's a cowboy or a prospector. And if I'm wrong, Duke, I hope you still got enough left inside you to run."

He pulled out his Winchester carbine from his saddle boot and made sure it was ready to fire. If it were Apache, they would not feel obliged to wait until he was ready to exchange greetings.

Clint cradled the Winchester in the crook of his arm. He was famous for his speed and accuracy with a Colt .45. But there were more than a few dead outlaws who'd made the mistake of thinking the Gunsmith was only average with a rifle. He wasn't—not by a long shot.

TWO

There was something about the smell of roasting horse that made Clint's stomach flop. Duke could tell the difference too. Apache. No doubt about it. Clint swore silently. They were still camped a good two miles ahead, down in an arroyo where he couldn't see them. But they were there all right. There might be one, or ten or fifty. Some of these arroyos and dry ravines were big enough to hide a wagon train.

Clint stopped Duke and thought carefully. He knew that there wasn't an Indian pony alive that could keep up with Duke, not for one mile or fifty. And Broken Lance had to be just less than three or four hours away. Clint studied the valley. It was a good fifteen miles wide and there were big-shouldered mountains bordering it on both the east and west. Hard, lifeless-looking mountains that looked like they had never felt rain. But there'd be springs up on those slopes, and wild animals—and Apache would know where to find them.

How many Apache? he wondered. If there were just a few, he'd skirt the arroyo close, but if there was a bunch, he knew he should head for one or the other of those mountain ranges.

Clint decided to take a chance and skirt the Apache

close. Maybe they'd be so busy roasting the horse that they'd never notice his passing.

"Easy, boy," he whispered to Duke. "I don't like the smell of it either, but short of you breaking a leg, there is no way they can catch us."

He rode ahead cautiously, flanking the plume of smoke by a good two miles and knowing that he was safe. If the Apache boiled out of the arroyo this very minute he would still be fine. But even so, Clint sort of wished now that he had stayed to the stage line road. Not that Apache considered that off-limits, hell no. In their minds, anything was fair game. This was their land, had been for untold centuries and it would stay theirs no matter how many reservations or treaties the white man made. Still, Clint thought, being near the stage line would have been more of a comfort.

As he came abreast of the smoke plume, Clint grew even more vigilant. The arroyo twisted so much he could not look up it and see anything but brush-choked banks. That was expected. Now, he rode down into it and started up the other side. Let them see me, he thought, relaxing just a little because a chase now would take him in the direction he wanted to go.

"Jesus God!" A man's tortured scream split the desert silence. He screamed again and then cried out in Spanish, "Don't do that to her any more!"

And then Clint heard the woman's cry of pain and outrage. It cut at the Gunsmith's soul like a jagged blade. She screamed again and again, and Clint halted Duke in the bottom of the arroyo and felt the sound beat at him. Everything he knew, all his intuition, every fiber in his body told him to ride on. His reasoning mind argued persuasively that the white man and woman captives were the same as dead—or if they weren't they wanted to be. Maybe the smell of flesh was theirs instead of horse. It damn sure wasn't beef.

"It's too late for them," he told himself angrily. Then, "Dammit, I'll never be able to hold my head up if I don't know for sure. A man loses his self-respect, he's dead and don't know it."

Clint reined Duke west to follow the deep, brush-choked arroyo toward the Apache camp. He guided Duke across the sandy parts so that the animal's iron shoes did not strike rock and warn of their approach. The screams had died as suddenly as they began and Clint felt this proved the pair were already dead. They must be, he thought. Time and time again he told himself to turn Duke around and ride the hell away because it was too late to help anyone except himself.

Once, when he was within a mile of the smoke, he did stop and silently debate the issue, but then he heard an anguished cry. It forced him to ride on. A half mile from the smoke, Clint dismounted and led Duke forward until he began to hear the Indians. The roasting meat and burning wood smells were thick and unwelcome to his nostrils.

Duke tossed his head nervously and Clint stopped to soothe the big gelding. Then they moved cautiously ahead until Clint was certain he was within a hundred yards of the Apache. He tied Duke to a piece of creosote brush and went ahead on foot.

Instinct told him the next bend in the arroyo would bring him into full view of the Apache camp. Clint crouched and pressed forward, feeling his heart slamming against his ribs. He placed each boot down carefully. Rifle ready, Colt loose in his holster, he figured that he could get off a minimum of four bullets before they could return fire.

He dropped and slithered the last few feet and when he stopped, he pushed a piece of sage out of his field of vision and met a blood-chilling sight. Two white men were lying spread-eagled against the bank of the arroyo. One was dead, the other surely wished to be. They had been mutilated, no doubt slowly, by the Apache. Scalped alive, their bodies were a mass of dark blood. Right now, the living one was having his ears removed—slowly. Mercifully, he was barely conscious. But the Apache would find ways to revive him for a moment's agony. Clint counted eight Apache.

Clint's eyes darted to the naked woman. Clearly, she had already been raped over and over. The humiliation would go on until she died or was killed. Neither possibility was far off. Right now, she was conscious but too weak to fight. At least that's what Clint thought until another Apache knelt between her legs. The moment he touched her, the woman screamed again and clawed feebly for his eyes.

The Apache rocked back on his haunches and said something to his friends. From their reaction, Clint had the impression they were admiring the poor young woman's spirit as well as her body. Maybe they would make her their slave and spare her life. She was dark and still attractive despite the torture. Apache respected courage, if nothing else. And this cruelty was no worse than what vicious white invaders had done to captured Indian squaws during years of murderous border warfare. Clint raised his Winchester and aimed at the man who now began to drive himself into the struggling woman. The Winchester roared and its slug knocked the Apache off the woman. For one split second, the Indians froze and in that instant of time, two more died. Then they were throwing themselves at him, not bother-

ing to go for their own rifles. Clint wounded a fourth,
then dropped his rifle and drew his Colt in one unbe-
lievably smooth motion that ended in fire and death.
Two more Apache died in midair after launching themselves at Clint and one of them landed on his gun hand,
pinning it to the rocky earth.

The last two surviving Apache figured the game was
over and threw themselves at Clint with a scream of bit-
ter revenge. Clint tore his hand loose but without the
Colt. He grabbed the first Apache's wrist and managed
to deflect the knife that was blurring toward his chest.
The Apache's body landed on him, but not before Clint
twisted the warrior's blade upward and sent it plunging
into the man's heart.

It was the last lucky Apache who would have him
pinned and defenseless. The Indian howled, knocked
Clint's Stetson aside and grabbed him by the hair. Clint
looked up into the man's dull, brutal eyes and faced
death. He saw the Apache's arm draw back and then the
man's knife slashed downward at his face. Clint twisted
his head sideways and felt the steel dig a long furrow
just over his left ear. For an instant, he almost lost con-
sciousness. The Apache, grinning now and sinking his
short, powerful fingers into Clint's throat, prepared to
drive his knife down into the eye socket.

A rifle boomed and the Apache shuddered. The
fingers in Clint's throat lost their steel grip and Clint
managed to tear his own arm free and drive it up into
the Apache's face. But the blow was weak and without
force. Ordinarily, the Apache would have easily
knocked Clint's fist aside and finished his work. But the
rifle boomed once more in the tight confines of the arroyo and the warrior grunted softly and died.

Clint shoved him aside and twisted his head around to

see the girl. Naked, swaying on her feet, bloodied, she looked like an avenging angel. Clint saw now that she was dark skinned, Mexican rather than white. He touched the wound along the side of his scalp, and felt the hot wet blood in his hair. He tried to roll to his knees and stand up. The girl saw one more Apache who was not quite dead and the rifle in her hands spoke.

Clint couldn't tear his eyes away from the woman.

She hadn't even aimed her rifle. But it was her expression and the look in her eyes that captured all of his attention. Her eyes were wild, tortured and fierce, like those of a feral animal. A creature you could never wholly trust, who would always be untamed. He wondered if she would kill him too.

He tried to stand up, failed. He tried to smile, but it must have been a poor attempt because the girl did not smile back. Instead, he stared with shock as she raised the weapon and aimed it at him. Jesus, Clint thought, she has gone mad. It's not that I blame her given what they did, but this is a damn poor way of thanking a man for. . . .

The rifle spat fire and flame and behind him, a mortally wounded Apache who had been trying to lift his knife now sighed and moved no more.

"Why you come?" the woman said with a Spanish accent as she lowered the rifle and moved to stand over Clint.

Ordinarily, it would have been a sight that would have revived almost any man from the dead. But not now. Not after what she had just gone through. Clint tried to stand but when he did, the arroyo's steep dirt walls began to move around and around. The last thing he remembered he was pitching over a dead Apache.

THREE

He awoke to a rough nudge and a drop of scalding fat that burned his cheek. Clint's eyes flew open and he saw the young woman leaning over him. She was dressed now, her face scratched and swollen, but clean. Her long black hair was brushed and tied back at her neck. She was kneeling over him holding a knife with a chunk of roasted horsemeat.

The sun was shining behind her and it made it seem as if she wore a golden halo although Clint suspected this woman was far from being an angel. Once more, as he looked into her eyes, he saw the flinty hardness. This was no city girl, but a woman born and bred to tough land and tough people.

"You eat." It was not a request, but a command.

"I don't stomach horsemeat," he said, pushing the blackened morsel aside and attempting to sit up. That was a big mistake. His head seemed to split down the middle and a jolt of pain made him groan.

"You live," she announced. "Not bad hurt."

"Thanks, I guess," he replied, squeezing his eyes shut and opening them again until he no longer saw double. He managed to climb to his feet but it was a struggle and he was weak as a kitten.

"Where you go?"

"My horse. I left him tied down the arroyo aways."

"We get him later."

"Now," Clint said between clenched teeth.

"You sit. I get horse."

Clint staggered. He turned and decided that was a fair idea. He was not up to walking even a quarter of a mile. It seemed altogether more intelligent to let the girl bring Duke to the camp.

While he waited for her, Clint surveyed the battlefield. Dead Apache all over the place. He was almost relieved to see that the second scalped captive had died. The man had suffered enough and now his slow execution was mercifully ended.

There were two animals that barely resembled horses. The pathetic creatures were nothing but skin and bones. Their heads hung low and they both looked worse than Clint felt. They'd probably have been roasting over the fire before the next week passed. There were three good repeating rifles and two old .44 Army cap-and-ball pistols that looked serviceable. He pushed a blanket aside and saw two more pistols and they were fine weapons, Colt .45s, both well-oiled and rigged for speed rather than accuracy. Clint figured the girl had gathered all this artillery together while he was unconscious. That was to be expected. There were a few filthy blankets and packs, two bows and quivers filled with arrows. Not much of anything else except three pretty fair Spanish saddles.

The girl returned leading Duke. She looked furious. "What matter with this stupid horse!" she demanded. "He no let me ride!"

"He's trained that way," Clint said, relieved to see Duke again. He walked over to him and patted his neck.

The horse seemed equally pleased to see the Gunsmith for it nuzzled his shoulder affectionately.

"Dumb horse."

"Smart as they come," Clint said retrieving his Stetson and then untying his canteen and giving the animal another drink.

The woman watched. "Horse can wait."

Clint didn't even bother to look up. He was beginning to think this girl might have a little Apache blood in her—she sure had their philosophy when it came to horses. She looked fully capable of shooting Duke for being the least bit uncooperative.

She strengthened this view by going over to the fire and cutting off another piece of horsemeat. She devoured it with relish and sliced off a second chunk. When her hunger was satisfied, she licked her fingers clean.

"If you're finished gorging yourself, I think we ought to get the hell out of here," Clint said.

The woman shook her head emphatically and pointed up at the blazing sun. "Too hot now. We wait until night, then ride."

"Not me," Clint said. "I want out of this death pit." He tightened the girth with effort, but when he tried to get his boot in the stirrup, the world began to spin again. He lost his balance, fell heavily but did not pass out. He knew that he must have lost quite a bit of blood to be so weak and dizzy. And even if he could get mounted, it made no sense to try and cross this desert at midday.

"You should eat," the girl said. "Make strong again."

Clint grimaced and grabbed the stirrup, using it to haul himself up to his feet. In his saddlebags there was

some antelope jerky and he'd eat that or even sad-
dleleather, before he'd eat roasted horse.

Clint found the jerky and sat down in the shade of his
horse. He didn't want to be here worth a damn but here
he would stay until it cooled this evening down into the
ninety-degree range. He bit into the jerky watching the
girl lead the two skeletal horses over near Duke and then
sit crosslegged in their shade.

He drank from his canteen and felt a little better.
"What's your name?"

"Juanita Sanchez," she told him. "You?"

"Clint Adams."

"Plenty good with gun and rifle."

He touched the wound along his scalp. "Not quite
good enough."

"You save me. I help you. What you want? More
guns? Horses? What?"

"I don't need any more guns and those horses are the
same as dead."

"OK, you let me know when you decide."

Clint tried to figure this woman out. Not sure if
Juanita was Indian or Mexican, or both. She treated
hardship and horses like an Apache and yet . . . she was
taller and much more attractive to him than a typical
Apache squaw. Her face was shaped more like his own,
the nose high rather than wide and flat. She was either
damned good looking and well built, or else the sun had
gotten to him and he didn't yet know it.

"There's no need, but thanks, anyway. What happened out here?"

In her own blunt, abbreviated way with English,
Juanita slowly told him that she was the daughter of
Manual Escobar Sanchez who had a large ranch down
in Mexico near a town and a river called Magdelena.

"I've heard of it. You're a long, hard road from home. What are you doing up here north of the border?"

"We hunt Geronimo. Find brother. Take back."

"Geronimo took your brother away?"

She nodded. "Him only ten. Mother, father very sad. Older brothers dead now."

When she said that, her eyes shifted toward the two men the Apache had scalped and mutilated.

Clint dropped his jerky in the dirt. "Those were your brothers?"

Again, just the faint nod of her head, though he thought he saw a shine in her eyes now. "Manuel and Gregorio. I shoot Gregorio."

Clint swallowed drily. Looking at her stiff face, the jaws locked together so tightly the muscles stood out in her cheeks, Clint understood that she had granted her brother's wish and shot him in order to end his agony. Involuntarily, Clint reached out to touch the woman in sympathy.

Juanita recoiled. "I do good thing, not bad," she said loudly. "Good thing, not bad!"

"Yeah," he agreed, "you do good thing, very brave thing, Juanita. Brother thank you. Clint admire you."

She relaxed and her eyes changed so that instead of them looking like obsidian, they grew a little soft to remind him of coal. It wasn't a change many men would have read, but Clint did. "Where do you want to go now?" he asked.

She pointed south. "Geronimo run to Mexico fast from soldiers. I find some day by damn."

"Why don't you go home after we bury your brothers?" he said. "Tell your mother and father that it is over. If you're the last of the Sanchez children, they'll need you when they grow very old and tired. Get married. Give them grandchildren.''

"Shut up," she said very distinctly. "Juanita find Geronimo and brother first!"

"All right. Your funeral. Were these some of his men?" Clint waved his hand at the dead Apache.

She shrugged.

"Do you know how far it is to Broken Lance?" He pointed to the southeast.

She held up nine fingers.

"Does that mean hours or miles?"

Apparently she did not know those words because she shrugged again, lay down and went to sleep.

Clint watched her. He had never met any woman like her. Daughter of a rancher, huh? That could mean anything from a rich man to one who ran a couple of goats in the sagebrush and had a chicken or two. Clint suspected that Juanita's father fit somewhere in the middle. The two good Colt pistols and rifles had probably belonged to them and their Mexican saddles were sound and well made. But on the other hand, Juanita Sanchez was far too hard to have been raised gentle. No wealthy Mexican rancher would send his own sons and daughter on such a dangerous mission. Instead, he would hire killers and offer a huge reward for the return of his son.

Clint wished he could help this young woman, or at least get her back to her parents so they could see that it was suicide for anyone to be knocking around in country alone like this. She had already been nearly raped to death, it would happen again if they caught her.

But what can I do? She told me to shut up and mind my own business. You can't tell a woman like Juanita anything.

Clint shook his head knowing it was hopeless. If Juanita Sanchez had it fixed in her head to keep after Geronimo and his renegade Apache band, she was as good as dead or a slave and there was no telling which was worse.

The Gunsmith lay down in the sand and closed his eyes. "Don't go wandering off now," he said to Duke, "but as the sun moves, kind of keep me in your shade until I wake up."

The horse stomped its feet as if it understood. The day grew hotter, flies buzzed over the dead and the fire stayed alive, fed by dripping grease from the charred haunch of roasting horsemeat.

FOUR

Clint had overslept and the sun was falling into the western horizon when he awoke feeling a whole lot better than when he had gone to sleep. He heard the woman grunting and when he rolled over, he saw her dragging Gregorio's body toward a grave she must have spent hours digging with nothing except maybe a stick and her bare hands.

He walked over to her and started to grab Gregorio's arm but something in Juanita's eyes changed his mind. So he let her bury her own brothers in a common grave while he whittled a cross out of two pieces of brush. It wasn't much of a cross, just two sticks that he bound together. Sort of smoothed out and with their initials carved into the wood. But when she saw it, she did something that moved him deeply. She took the cross and kissed his hands, both of them, and then gave him what had to be a blessing.

Clint wasn't a real religious man, but he did believe in a higher power than himself. Juanita obviously did too, because tears sprang into her eyes. She took his hand in her own and they walked over to the grave. She placed the cross down into the heavy sand and then knelt and prayed. Watching her, Clint was reminded how many

21

sides a woman could have. Watching her eat, or fight
with her last ounce of strength, you'd have thought she
was a wildcat without any deep softness to her at all.
But now, bent and praying, her face bathed in the glow
of the desert sunset, Clint was humbled by her faith and
beauty. He resolved to try once more to talk her into
going home, perhaps with a force of heavily armed men
already riding that way.

While Clint hauled big rocks to cover the grave and
keep the coyotes from digging up the brothers, Juanita
quickly packed everything of value on one of the
Apache ponies and let it be understood that she hoped
to use the weapons to trade for her little brother.
Winchester rifles and good pistols were worth more
than human lives in some parts of Mexico—at least to
the banditos and the Apache. Problem was, there was
no need for those kinds of men to trade—they just took
whatever they wanted in this desolate land because
nobody was going to stop them.

When they rode out of the arroyo, Clint was mighty
glad to be putting behind the smell of roasting horse and
dead men. Overhead, vultures circled low in the dusky
light.

"You coming with me into Broken Lance?" he
asked.

She nodded. "Trade for supplies."

"Good."

"I stay with you, Clint."

"Yes, I'll look after you in Broken Lance."

It was still hot, but once the sun went down it cooled
real fast. Juanita's weak Indian ponies moved as though
they were walking through knee-deep sand. But Clint
wasn't complaining, because they saw the lights of
Broken Lance long before midnight. Nine fingers had

meant nine miles, not nine hours, and Clint was damn glad.

They rode into a darkened livery and Clint had to bang on the barn door for about five minutes before the owner came out pulling on his trousers and notching his suspenders over his sloping shoulders. He was heavyset, in his mid-thirties, hard-looking and not very happy about being awakened.

"What the. . . ." The words died in his mouth when he saw Juanita and her two Apache ponies. "Jesus!" He spat. "If you think I'm going to take in those two bags-o-bones you're plain loco. The black, sure. But not those two Indian ponies. Tell your squaw to get them mangy critters outta here!"

Clint dismounted. He was hot, dirty, stumbling with hunger and his head wound throbbed. And now he was seething. There was nothing that made him angrier than a lack of compassion for sick or weak animals. Those two ponies sure as hell had not wanted to be starved into their present condition. They had been cruelly mistreated and pushed almost to their limits but they had never quit trying to please. That made them gallant in Clint's eyes. And even though he probably could not save them from their eventual fates with the Apache, it had given him no small measure of joy in knowing he was going to reward the poor buggers with at least one night of earthly paradise. Individual stalls, clean straw, lots of good grass hay, and all the oats they could safely handle without foundering—yes, and all the clean, cool water that they wanted.

But now, this big, dumb sonofabitch was sending these horses away. There might be other liveries in town, but maybe not, because Broken Arrow was pretty small. Clint looked at the man who outweighed him by twenty-five pounds and said, "You're going to give all three horses the best this place has got to give. I'm paying for the best so you're delivering."

"The hell with that! Get them two outta here!"

Clint could see that the man had his mind set in the wrong direction. He could also see that a big, strapping fella like this probably only understood force and that kindness to dumb animals was totally beyond the grasp of his limited mentality. That's why Clint saved his breath and punched the liveryman instead. Punched him so hard it sent the man backpedaling into the barn and crashing in the darkness.

Clint sucked on a cut knuckle. He had to remember that teeth cut and broke hands. The Gunsmith needed his hands in good working order.

Juanita looked down at him. "Man done?"

"I wish he was. But I just don't think that's the case. Give him about half a minute and he'll make his appearance."

Clint had it figured right. Thirty seconds later the liveryman came roaring out of the barn, arms outstretched with every intention of getting Clint in a bearhug and breaking his spine. Clint had other ideas. Knowing that he was in no shape to endure a tough fist fight, he waited until the man was almost on top of him. At the last possible instant, he stepped aside drawing his gun and bringing its barrel slashing down across the man's forehead. The fight was over.

Juanita stepped down and smiled. "Clint smart hombre."

He had to laugh at that. Tonight, he would do the feeding and he'd bind the liveryman up and toss him into an empty stall so he didn't get crazy and take his unhappiness out on their horses. Tomorrow, he'd ask

Ed Brisco for a better place to board their animals.

It was two in the morning before they staggered into the hotel lobby. Clint was out on his feet and so was Juanita. He looked around for a night clerk, saw none, and went to the key board and selected two that were hanging side by side on pegs.

"It's been a rough day, Miss Sanchez. Let's get some good sleep and talk things over tomorrow. Maybe you'll change your mind about going off alone into Mexico."

She took the key and followed him up the steps. He unlocked both rooms and struck a match in each to make sure that they were empty. Then, he showed Juanita into hers and gave her the key.

Clint moved toward the bed. Despite the fact that he had slept most of the day, he still felt exhausted and weak from the loss of blood. He was going to sleep.

FIVE

Clint awoke to Juanita's soft knock on the door.

"Clint, I'm afraid to be alone tonight. I come sleep next to you?"

"Uh, sure. Come on in." Clint wondered how he was going to resist touching this beautiful woman. He didn't have to. Juanita crawled in beside him, dressed in a white cotton shift. "Oh, Clint, it feel good to be near man I can trust." Clint smiled ruefully in the dark.

The bed was not built for two people, and Clint and Juanita were lying very close when she said, "Clint, I want to kiss you." Clint was surprised. Things happened pretty quickly after that.

Juanita's skin was moist and she smelled of soap instead of sweat the way he still did. She looked cool, too. Her breasts were large and firm, they shone wetly in the moonlight and her nipples were big and dark. Clint could not help worrying about maybe hurting her after what she had been through.

After they had kissed for a long while, Juanita pulled off her shift. She was completely naked underneath. Her V-shaped crotch was thick with curly black hair and smelled of soap too. She was lithe and slim with all the curves in all the right places. Her hand closed around his

stiff manhood and he got even stiffer until his erection
stood up proud as a flagpost.

She lowered her head and took him inside of her
mouth and began to suck. Slow at first, then more and
more avidly. He remembered how she had devoured the
roasting horsemeat like a wild animal. Now she was
doing almost the same to him. And he couldn't stop
her—didn't want to stop her. Perhaps, he thought, she
was trying to obliterate the memory of the Apache by
making love to him.

When his legs began to tremble, he heard her soft
laughter. "What's so funny?" he managed to ask.

"Maybe you like better than this, Clint?" she said,
climbing up to lower herself onto his throbbing, glisten-
ing staff. He let her settle down real slow and easy and
he held his breath not wanting to hurt her because he
knew she had to be very sore.

"Nope," he said feeling himself slipping inside of
her, "this is going to be even better."

He felt her womanhood settle down tight over him,
taking him in all the way and then beginning to bump in
and out.

Her mouth closed over his own and then he was kissing her fiercely. Their tongues played together and their
bodies began to slam together nice and easy at first, then
quickly rougher. This was not going to be a delicate ses-
sion of lovemaking, but then, Juanita Sanchez wasn't a
delicate woman.

He rolled her over onto her back and let his body
teach her what it was like to be loved by the Gunsmith.
Their bodies beat at each other, just as their wills had
when they'd first met. Clint clenched his teeth and drove
in and out until her fingers grabbed his buttocks and
began pulling him at her in a frenzy.

She threw her head back and her legs began to flay the sheets as she lost control. Dimly, he wondered if any man had ever made her climax and he knew that, after this moment, she would demand it every time.

Juanita's animal scream began deep in her throat and he felt it coming up from her as her body began bucking like a horse that had never been ridden before. He covered her mouth with his own and stifled her yell with his groan of passion. It was like a volcano going off when they came, his seed pumping deep into her hungry body, her every muscle milking him over and over until he lay dry and exhausted.

"You hell of a hombre, Clint Adams," she said happily. "We do again very soon. I go to Mexico come the sun, and find my brother."

He nodded weakly and laid his head on her heaving breasts. "Yeah," he said hoarsely, "But I sure wish I could change your stubborn mind, and not go alone."

He began to suck on her breasts, teasing them with his lips and teeth. She responded eagerly. Clint was hoping maybe he could change her mind—not by reason or argument, but by doing what he was doing to her now. They made love once more. But this time it was gentler, passionate but more relaxed.

SIX

Sometime just before dawn, Clint dozed. He hadn't intended to, but there was no doubt that the loss of blood and the strenuous but highly pleasurable night with Juanita had left him drained. He awoke hearing a rooster crow somewhere and his hand moved out to touch the Mexican girl.

She was gone. Clint was instantly alert. He sat up quickly and studied the room. She was really gone. He jumped out of bed and dressed quickly, then hurried down the stairs into the empty lobby. Clint knew where she was going and he headed for the livery stable.

He was too late. The two Apache ponies were missing along with all of the weapons. "Dammit!" Clint cussed in anger.

Duke nickered softly and Clint went over to scratch the animal's ears. "I don't think we'll ever see Miss Sanchez again," he said, remembering the feel of that woman, her courage and passion. "But I sure won't forget her easily."

A banging sound and muffled grunts sent Clint into the next stall where the liveryman lay in the semi-darkness. He hadn't had much luck untying himself during the night. Clint could see the man was damned angry. He'd probably grab a pitchfork and want to kill him and Duke.

"The hell with you," Clint said to the man who thrashed around in the straw gagged and trussed up like a calf at branding time. "You can just wait until someone else comes along. I don't feel in the mood to shoot you this morning."

He pitched a silver dollar at the man that more than paid him for the feed bill. Then, he brushed and saddled Duke and rode off looking for another livery. From the noises that man had been making, Clint figured he might have poisoned Duke in spite. It wasn't worth taking chances. There were a lot of crazy people running loose on the frontier. Maybe the liveryman would come hunting him, but he would take care of that problem if it came and in its own good time.

Clint found another livery and he rode wide around it checking out the condition of the boarded horses. Satisfied that they were fat and well brushed, he figured he would bring Duke back there later. But for now, he wanted to see Ed Brisco and buy him a breakfast. It would be mighty nice seeing his old friend and mentor. Ed had taught him a lot of necessary tricks to staying alive. And a lot of wisdom too. Things like not taking outlaws too personally but treating each one like a job rather than a crusade. Crusaders took foolish chances and got killed early in their careers.

Broken Lance was only about fifteen businesses long on Main Street. It looked just like a hundred other border towns. Tough. Dry. Hard-scrabble. There was a small plaza and it was shaded by some droopy-looking cottonwoods that looked thirsty. Most of the buildings were made of wood or adobe and had the stamp of the southwest all over them. Clint had been down in Mexico a time or two and you could tell that Broken Lance was about half Mexican, half American. Once again, Clint wondered why Ed had chosen to live here.

It took Clint all of two minutes to find the sheriff's office. When there were only fifteen businesses on each side of the street, you could cover them pretty fast, especially when about a third were either saloons or hotels that doubled as whore houses.

Clint tied Duke up in front of the sheriff's office and stepped up on the boardwalk. A mangy but still powerful old dog with ragged ears moseyed up to him, wagging its whip-like tail. Clint patted its head. The dog beat at his leg with the almost hairless tail and then trotted along the walk. It stopped at about every other post it came to and raised its leg to mark its territory.

Clint tried the door and it was locked. Not surprising. A sheriff kept damn late hours. Same as bartenders and gamblers. Fortunately, there was never much trouble in the early morning so he could sleep in. Might be as late as ten before he got up, knowing he'd be out on the streets until well after midnight. For a married man, the hours and the dangers were hell, but for a bachelor, it was all right. Clint had always been single and a night owl. It was only during the last couple of years that he could go to bed before midnight certain he could sleep.

Clint looked inside but the place was empty. Stomach growling loudly, Clint twisted around and studied the street. Already, people were starting to get ready for the day. He saw shopowners going to work and men heading for one of two different cafes to eat their breakfast. Clint guessed he would go along and eat with them. He could always buy Ed lunch and dinner—if the man had recovered enough from his gunshot. It occurred to him that Ed might have gotten married and

Clint hoped so because nothing needed looking after more than an old lawman.

The cafe was filling up fast and Clint ordered coffee, a steak and fried potatoes. Eggs were fifty cents apiece so he decided to pass them up. The coffee came fast, good and strong the way he liked. The steak and potatoes were right on the coffee's heels and the waitress who brought them had a nice smile. It melted though, when she saw the side of his scalp.

"What in the blue blazes happened to your head?" she asked.

Clint was so famished that he did not want to explain. Besides, if he told her the truth—that he'd killed seven or eight Apache—then pretty soon the news would be all over the cafe, then the town. People got real upset every time anything happened to an Apache—good or bad.

Their reasoning sort of went like this: if you killed an Apache, that was real good—but also real bad. Good because they all hated Apache but bad because the Apache hated them back—and they put revenge right at the top of their priorities. An eye for an eye and a tooth for a tooth it said in the Bible. Well, the Apache carried that a few horrible steps further. So if you killed one, at least one poor white or Mexican was going to pay hell and lose his scalp. More than likely, so too would his entire family or any unfortunate friends who happened to be around.

"Well, sir, you aren't much for talking, but you sure act hungry," the waitress said. "Better have another steak."

He nodded. "Not quite so bloody this time around."

"Burn one!" the waitress yelled at the kitchen.

Clint ate the second steak a lot slower. He realized that he had not eaten a good meal since Tucson two and a half days earlier. No wonder his belt was drawn up another notch.

He signaled for his fourth cup of coffee and felt almost human again.

"I never saw a man put the grub away like you, mister." The waitress studied him carefully. "You're new in town, aren't ya?"

"Just arrived today."

"You came to find gold like all these other?"

"Nope. I'm an old friend of Sheriff Ed Brisco." Clint lifted his coffee cup to drink. "You know what time he checks into his office?"

"Died about this time yesterday, mister. They're burying poor Ed this morning. You want any more of this coffee?"

Clint set his cup down hard and stared at his greasy plate. All the noise in the busy cafe sort of went out the window as the impact of her words hit him like a mule-kick to the stomach.

"You all right?"

He nodded. Swiveled off his stool and paid his bill, then walked outside to steady himself against a hitching rail and Duke. Sonofabitch, he thought, feeling miserable all of a sudden. Ed was gone. Backshot. Getting planted in this godforsaken desert.

How old had he been? Fifty? Not much over that. But that was old for a frontier sheriff in a town where the dregs came to get rich or escape justice in the big towns. Clint remembered once how Ed Brisco had earned his reputation by stepping out in a Wyoming cattletown street one snowy afternoon to halt a bank robbery. They say he'd used his Winchester like it was a musical instrument only instead of notes, he played bullets. Ed had three bullet wounds in his body. Clint had seen them.

But five very dangerous bank robbers had died that day, and Ed had saved the town from going bankrupt. They'd given him their thanks and drinks on the house.

Backshot. Some cowardly sonofabitch had got him from ambush. Even at fifty, Ed would still have been oil-smooth with a sixgun and rock-steady. The man had lived a good life, he had kept himself in shape and had always bragged he would live to be at least seventy.

A full-bearded miner started to pass him going into the cafe and Clint said, "You know Sheriff Brisco?"

"Never heard of him! This town got a sheriff? You sure wouldn't have knowed it last night, by God! We raised a little hell, you bet. Like to pulled Broken Lance down to kindling wood!"

"Where's the funeral parlor?"

"Beats the hell out me. And I don't give a damn."

He passed on, leaving Clint to wonder how much difference any lawman ever made. Dead one day and the town was going to hell already. People didn't deserve any justice. They obeyed the law out of fear—not respect.

"Mister," Clint said, with rising anger in his voice, to another man passing, "where's the damned funeral parlor?"

The man looked at him. "Five doors down on this side of the street," he said, hurrying past.

Clint nodded and started down the boardwalk. If the undertaker wasn't in yet, Clint would bust in the door. He should have found Ed a whole lot sooner. Maybe if he had, he could have talked the man into going somewhere other than this hell hole of a town.

SEVEN

Clint peered through the window and saw the undertaker moving around inside. He banged on the door.

"I'm not open yet," the undertaker said peevishly.

"You are for me," Clint replied. He pushed inside, ignoring the undertaker's shrill protest.

Ed was dressed in a good suit but lying in a cheap pine box. "I want him buried in a coffin," Clint said. "Get him out of that thing! He wasn't any unwashed, unsung two-bit gunslinger. That's Ed Brisco and he deserved the best."

The undertaker looked twice at Clint. "Payment in advance for our deluxe coffin, complete with satin lining and . . . ."

Clint spun around wanting to hit the man. He put his hand in his pocket. "Here's a hundred dollars. The best you've got or I'll come back here after the funeral and someone might just have to make arrangments for you. I want a marble headstone. Biggest one you have."

"But sir! That takes time to carve and is an additional expense."

Clint grabbed the man by the coat front and shook him as a terrier would a rat. "You do it today, or face the consequences. Understand?"

"All right! All right!"

Clint shoved him aside. "Now leave me alone with him for a minute."

While he did not mean to be hard-nosed or excessively rough, undertakers, morticians as they preferred to be called, were a breed that the Gunsmith just didn't have much use for. They profited from misery. They profited hugely. Clint had dealt with one hell of a lot of the bastards, and he had never met one he liked.

Alone, Clint looked down at the face seeing how Ed hadn't changed all that much. The man still had that lean and chiseled jawline, the sharp nose and the incisive features that gave evidence of a well-disciplined mind. Ed had always been the best judge of men and evidence that Clint had ever known. But someone had killed him and unless Clint was very mistaken, it had been unexpected. Why and who? Those were the questions that Ed had always challenged himself and his deputies with.

"I'll stay here and find out," Clint promised. "I swear that I will bring your murderer to justice."

Saying that, Clint steeled his nerves and lifted Ed out of his pine box. He turned the man over and peeled up his coat and shirt to study the bullet holes. There were three of them, right up high and all closely spaced between the shoulder blades. It was good aim by any standard and it had been fast because Ed would have started to turn when the first bullet punched into his body. Clint dug a knife out of his pocket and took a deep breath. He'd only need one of the slugs and he was sure that they'd be .45 caliber like everyone used, but sometimes a gun left its own mark on a bullet. Not often, but sometimes.

Five minutes later he left the room satisfied he could learn no more from the body. "The funeral is at ten?"

The mortician nodded sullenly.

"Where's Boot Hill?"

"The Broken Lance Cemetery is a half mile south of town," the man snipped. He was tall and anemic looking, just the right type for this line of work. This one reminded Clint of a parasite. Some kind of a beetle.

"I'll be there and don't be late." He wrote down what he wanted on the tombstone, slammed the door and stalked down the boardwalk. It was too early to drink, but he felt like a shot of whiskey anyway. The saloons would be open by now and already starting to get busy. Often as not, a lawman could learn more during a few hours of hanging around a saloon than he could in a month of asking official questions.

He entered the first saloon he came to and ordered a shot of whiskey—the good stuff. The whiskey tasted fine. It replaced the pain in his head with a nice fire in his belly. Clint ordered one more and left it untouched.

Back in Tucson, Pecos James had told him there was some kind of a range war, or big trouble down here, and Clint figured he could ask a few innocent-sounding questions and learn all about the situation.

He was not disappointed. There were a dozen men already in the saloon and everyone was talking about the murder of a man named Shorty Rye. It seemed that Shorty had been prospecting on the high mesa. And everyone knew the danger in crossing Covington range. Everyone, that is, except Clint.

"It's open range," a prospector spat. "But old Angus Covington swears he'll shoot trespassers."

"Who is he?"

"Biggest cattle and sheep rancher in this part of the state. The man claims most of the southeastern corner of Arizona. And nobody cared for years. But now that pockets of gold are being discovered out there, it's different."

"I see." Clint sipped his whiskey. "Why don't a judge decide if Covington has legal rights or not?"

"No judge is that stupid," another prospector said. "Covington is the law hereabouts. And he does have legal title to some of the land. Just not all of it like he claims."

"I see. Did Sheriff Brisco take a side to this?"

"Yep. The wrong one by the way he ended face down in the dirt."

Clint swallowed. "Which is that?"

"Our side, of course. The Sheriff, he couldn't be run off by the Covingtons. Or bought off either. He'd sworn to see that justice was done and look what they did to him."

"Any proof?"

"Yeah," a fiesty little prospector with bloodshot eyes and red hair hissed. "He's dead ain't he!"

Clint finished his whiskey. He left the saloon knowing a whole lot more than he'd known coming in. Apparently, this old man Covington was a real tyrant. A land baron who ruled his range as if he were a feudal lord. Those kind of men cared nothing for the law.

Clint went out to Duke. He would see who came to Ed's funeral—if anybody. Sometimes a man's death attracted not only his best friends but also his worst enemies.

The late Sheriff Edward Brisco had taught him that little lesson too.

EIGHT

Clint stood alone in the blazing sun, feeling the sweat trickle down his backbone and the sun burning the back of his wide shoulders. Ten o'clock, and his anger was starting to build. Lizards skittered around on the gravestones and hung upside down on ornamental iron fences that kept animals from the corpses. Broken pieces of whiskey bottles glinted amber like cat's eyes. A cemetery you wouldn't want to go to—not even dead.

Sonofabitch, Clint thought miserably, as two sweat-soaked and shaking workmen pitched shovels into a buggy and drove off to Broken Lance talking about how many beers they were going to drink with the undertaker's money.

He watched the hearse come rolling out from town and was surprised to see that it was followed by a carriage and two small buggies. Seeing that a few other people were coming to pay their respects raised Clint's spirits a little.

The carriage rolled in first and the undertaker had it backed up to the grave. He shot Clint a mean glance and then motioned for him and the driver to help get the casket out.

"I hope you approve."

"So do I," Clint said tersely as they rigged up ropes

39

and lowered it down into the hole.

When Clint straightened up, the other mourners were present, though some of them didn't look all that mournful. But a woman in her fifties who Clint guessed was either Mrs. Briscoe or Ed's old girlfriend was sobbing. She was matronly, but pretty too in a soft, comforting way. She had red-rimmed eyes and wore too much rouge on her cheeks but she looked kind and respectable. Like your mother should. Clint went over and introduced himself.

"He told me a lot about you," the woman sniffled. "And how come you're known as the Gunsmith."

At the mention of that name, the short old heavyset man blinked. He exchanged looks with his daughter and another man. All three stared at Clint with keen interest. Clint had a gut feeling that the older fella was Angus Covington. Covington looked important and somewhat hostile but his daughter just looked curious.

The girl was probably in her late twenties, about five-four with yellow hair and a darkly tanned face. She was wearing a dress, but under it, Clint saw a nice pair of polished riding boots. She was good-looking, with a strong face and wide-set inquiring eyes. She looked like what she was—a rancher's daughter with a lot of spit and fire. She was probably used to ordering men around, and she struck Clint as being the kind of young woman who'd enjoy that.

Returning his attention to the weeping woman, Clint said, "And who are you?"

"My name is Clair Morrison and I'm the woman who loved Ed," she blubbered, fixing her accusing eyes on the older man. "And you don't belong here, Mr. Covington! You had Ed murdered!"

Angus Covington flushed, which wasn't easy because his face was naturally red anyhow. Clint noted his quick temper and how his fists knotted at his side. "I respected Ed as much as any man I ever met," Covington said tightly. "If I wanted to kill him, I'd have tried it myself."

"Liar! Ed was a better man than you ever dreamed about being. He was honest and aboveboard. Something you never could be!"

"Now wait just a darn minute, Clair Morrison!" the girl shouted, stepping between Clair and her father. "I know that Father and Ed had gotten crosswise of each other on this range law business, but they were friends long before you ever came to Broken Lance!"

The tall man Clint's age took the girl's arm. "No need to get all het up, now Lucy. Clair sure didn't mean what she said."

"The hell I didn't, Earl Sturges! And you can just keep your nose plumb out of this altogether. I don't trust you any more than Angus!"

Earl was a handsome man with pale red hair and even paler blue eyes. He had a boyish scattering of freckles on his face and yet, he looked very tough and competent.

Clint decided it was time to break things up and give poor Ed a moment of peace before they tossed the dirt on his casket. "Who's going to read from the Bible?" he asked shortly.

"I will," Clair said, clearly ruffled and upset.

Clint tried to listen but gave up after a few minutes. The temperature must have been in the upper nineties already and heat waves were shimmering off the distant hills down south. He thought of Juanita Sanchez somewhere out there. He wondered if she was holed up in the shade of a cactus or if maybe she was already captured and dead. One thing sure, those two scarecrow ponies of hers would not outrun an Apache. He wished he'd figured out a way to stop her from going.

Clair Morrison finished the reading and gripped the Bible tightly. "Mr. Gunsmith," she said, voice near breaking, "I guess you'll want to say a few kind words over our dear departed Edward."

Clint started with surprise. He hadn't intended to say anything but now that he was on the spot, he reckoned he'd give it his best try. So he spoke about Ed, how the man had taken him under his wing and saved his bacon a time or two when he was maybe a hair's breadth faster but foolish. And how Ed had sort of been the father that he'd never had but dreamed about. And how Ed had taught him a bunch of gun tricks and then told him to forget them all because they were damned foolishness. Then, Clint remembered to tell these people how it was Ed who'd beat Clint out of his deputy's small wages playing poker, but how he'd learned to gamble with the best and figured that Ed deserved his money for being such a fine teacher.

Clint could have gone on and on for about an hour about all the things that Ed Brisco had done and taught him but when Miss Morrison passed out from the heat, he realized this was not the time or the place. So while they pitched in the dirt and held up Clair, the Gunsmith ended with, "All I have left to say is that I mean to find out who shot Ed and then see him hanged high."

"Praise the Lord!" Clair said, reviving momentarily. "And may his mangy killer rot in everlasting hell!"

The nice middle-aged couple who had brought Clair out took her back to town. Clint watched the buggy roll away, and decided that he needed to talk to the woman tomorrow when she was a little more rational.

"I didn't kill him, or order him killed," Angus Covington said gruffly. He was a barrel-chested banty rooster of a fellow. White haired, big white mustache and deep-set but honest blue eyes. Clint figured himself as a good judge of character and his initial reaction said that the man was telling the truth. "And any time you think you want to pull a rope over my neck, you come right at me man to man, Gunsmith. I'm not afraid of you or anyone else for that matter."

"He'd have to get by me first, Mr. Covington."

Clint looked closer at Earl Sturges. The man was well over six feet and rangy. He looked like he could whip his weight in wildcats. Still, there was no reason why he had to add that last remark unless he was out to impress the Covingtons.

"Be still, Earl," Lucy Covington said. "I'm sure the Gunsmith doesn't believe that father killed Ed Brisco, do you?"

"I don't know anything yet. Ed taught me to keep my mouth shut and my gun loose. He always said that was the best way to stay in whatever game I wanted to play. Right now, that seems like pretty good advice."

"Yeah," Angus said, watching the driver and the undertaker finish filling in the dirt and drag out the marble headstone. "Damn that's a pretty one," he said. "Lucy, I want one like that only bigger."

"Father! Can we discuss this some other time?"

The old rancher nodded. "Maybe it would be better said in the shade. Gunsmith, I'm going to take a gamble and invite you out to the ranch. If you stay in Broken Lance, those thieving miners are going to convince you that I'm a cold-blooded murderer. That I backshot poor Ed and that I ought to be hung by the balls or beat to death with cactus plants. That's all a bunch of bullshit. I homesteaded this land and I've been fighting to hold and keep it for twenty-four years. Those Johnny-come-latelies find a couple of gold nuggets on my range and suddenly, there's a gold rush down here. They shoot my

cattle and ruin my water holes. They befoul the land and
I won't have them on it.''

"Open range is open range," Clint said. "I sym-
pathize with you, but if you can't prove ownership . . .''

"Ownership! Why, I . . . .''

Lucy grabbed the man. "Father, it's not good to get
all upset in this heat. Let's go back to the ranch. You
and the Gunsmith can talk where it's cooler.''

"Might be a good idea," Clint said, feeling dizzy in
this heat.

"All right, then. Let's go. Earl, bring around the
other buggy and let the Gunsmith ride with us. He can
tie that black gelding of his to the back of the wagon.''
Angus pointed a thick finger at the headstone. "Just
like that one, Lucy. But plant me on the ranch under the
cottonwoods beside your Ma. I sure would hate to lie
here in this miserable hot bastard of a hillside.''

Clint shook his head. Even with the headstone and
the nice coffin, Ed Brisco deserved a good sight better.

As he started after Lucy and her father, Earl sort of
bumped up next to him and said in a low, ominous
voice, "You be civil or you'll get your ass whipped up
between your shoulders and I don't care how fast you
are with a sixgun.''

Clint would have grabbed the man but he was moving
away too fast. Clint scowled. He wondered what kind of
a burr was under Earl's saddle and then he figured it
out. The man was furious because someone else was
taking his seat beside the Covingtons.

Watch out for him, Clint told himself. He's a live
bullet in a hot fire just waiting to go off and kill someone foolish enough to get close to power and beauty.

NINE

It was a long, hot ride to the Covington Ranch, and without a canvas cover over the rig, Clint and the Covingtons would have fried. On the way to the ranch, Clint heard all about how Angus Covington had homesteaded this county, fought Apache so often he'd lost count of the number of skirmishes. After four decades of fighting, Angus and the non-warring Apache had sort of called a truce. Peaceable Apache were allowed to cross his land and each fall Angus took twenty head over to the reservation and gave them to the Indians as a token of friendship.

"But there are still a bunch of 'em that plague me and my boys all the time," he grumped. "The thing about Apache is that there are at least six tribes and they can't settle on any one leader. Every little band has its own boss and none of them agree on much of anything. Good thing for the whites. Hell, if Cochise had had even a hundred warriors, he'd still be around kicking the hell outta both the United States and Mexican armies. Apache hate whites, but they hate the Mexicans a damn sight more."

Clint thought about Juanita. "How come?"

"They just do. You see, a lot of Mexicans got Indian

blood, but they turned farmer. Apache can't stand people like us who claim land. To them, the land belongs to everyone and no one. You followin' me, Gunsmith?''

He nodded.

"Good. The Mexican government, it made a big mistake about fifty years ago when it placed a bounty on the Apache. One hundred pesos for a warrior's scalp, 50 for squaw and 25 for child—even a baby. Mexicans used to go after the kids, and the Apache never forgave them. Especially Geronimo. You know much about him?''

"Nope.'' Clint knew it did not matter whether or not he did, he was going to hear about the man anyway. And so Angus Covington told him how Geronimo's father had once been a chief of the Nedni Apache in northern Mexico but had forfeited that title when he married into the Mimbres Apache band.

"The way I figure it, Geronimo never forgave his daddy. You see, the only way an Apache can become a chief is if his daddy's one, or else he's so all-fired vicious he gets elected by the tribal council.''

"So Geronimo had to go that latter route.''

"Yep. But the Mexican state of Chihuahua sure helped when they invited the Mimbres to a peace council in the little town of Janos, down along the Sierra Madre.''

"And the Apache believed them?'' Clint knew how suspicious the Apache were.

"Not altogether,'' Angus said, "but they had a powwow and decided it was worth the risk to get the blankets, food and horses the Mexican government had promised them if they showed up. Cochise and Geronimo especially figured it was worth the danger. So they all went sorta expecting a trap."

Angus used his whip to make the horses trot faster. "But the Mexicans were clever. They acted peaceable enough. Talks were started and the Mexicans were promising that they'd drop the hated Apache scalp bounty. The Apache began to think the Mexican government was sincere. Every evening the Indian leaders rode back to their camp loaded down with new gifts and peace offerings."

"I see a trap coming," Clint said.

"Sure you do. By the end of the week, the military governor of Sonora had his soldiers encircle the Apache camp and then open fire on the women and the children while the Indian leaders were talking peace in Janos. It was slaughter. Geronimo's young wife and three kids were cut down in the first volley and they say the death count was 130, mostly children, squaws and old folks."

Clint shook his head. No wonder Geronimo hated the Mexicans!

Lucy Covington's face grew hard. "When Cochise, Geronimo and the other leaders returned to find their people had been slaughtered, they vowed to kill Mexicans whenever they could as long as they lived. And ever since that day, they have kept their word—to the horror of the poor villages in northern Mexico."

"Tell me about the gold rush down here," Clint said. "And about who you think might have killed Ed Brisco."

Lucy smiled. "You don't waste much time, do you, Gunsmith?"

"Not usually."

Lucy let her father answer. "Some sonofabitch snuck onto my range and hit a strike last year. Of course, he went back to Broken Lance, and then on to Tombstone and told everyone about it. He was murdered for his gold and deservedly so. Anyone fool enough to run around bragging about his gold doesn't deserve to live. They found the man's body and he'd been tortured. Seemed obvious that they'd tried to get the fool to tell them exactly where he struck paydirt."

"But he didn't?"

"Nope. All he ever said was that it was on my cattle and sheep range. Do you know how many acres it takes down here to feed one cow?"

"A hell of a lot, I'll bet."

"About fifty, and it'd be more except that I have some high desert land south of here right up against the Chiricahua Mountains that is damn good cattle country. It ain't near as much as I need, but it helps plenty. I summer my livestock up in the mountains and winter them on the desert below. Somehow, we get by."

"So I hear," Clint said drily. From the talk in the saloon, old Angus Covington got along pretty darn well.

"Ain't much more than a living, I'll tell you. We got damn little to show for the years we been here and the risks we took. Lost Lucy's mother after she was bit by a rattler. Four sons ambushed and tortured to death by the Apache. And now, Lucy's husband has been killed by some bushwhackin' prospector."

Clint was surprised. For some reason he had the impression that Earl Sturges had long ago staked his claim on Lucy Covington. "I'm sorry to hear that. Any idea who the killer was?"

"Not a clue," she said quietly. Lucy stared at her hands. "My husband was a man who made more than his share of enemies, Clint. You'll hear this sooner or later and I'd prefer you heard it from me. My husband was found shot to death in . . . . in a Tombstone brothel."

"The sonofabitch deserved it!" Angus swore vehemently.

Clint couldn't think of anything to say. He clamped his mouth shut and they traveled the rest of the way to ranch headquarters in heavy silence. The land did green up a mite as they climbed a long succession of foothills. And by the time they arrived at the ranch headquarters, Clint was prepared to say that, while this wasn't his favorite kind of country, it sure wasn't the hell he had ridden across when he'd come upon Juanita.

"There it is," Angus said proudly. "Home."

The old rancher had reason to be proud. The setting was pretty. Angus had chosen the site of a large artesian spring and there was plenty of water. Big cottonwood trees ringed the ranchyard and gave it a peaceful look of permanence. The outbuildings formed a semicircle. Bunkhouse, livery, barns, cookhouse, and various other buildings. And right in the middle of it all stood the adobe Covington ranch house. It was impressive: U-shaped with verandas and patios, it seemed part of the land. Clint could see Mexican domestic workers and their families and the small houses they lived in. There were huge corrals with both horses and cattle. Everything that Clint saw was in fine order. No busted boards on the barns, no holes needing patching on the roofs, no missing or even damaged poles in the round horse-breaking corrals. Angus Covington ran a tidy operation.

When they rolled into the yard, children waved and laughed and Lucy waved back. It occurred to Clint that

these were a happy people. That told you a lot about the
Covingtons. Clint guessed his first impression was cor-
rect, and that Angus wasn't responsible for Ed Brisco's
murder. A murderer was not the sort of man who
engendered great love and respect from his employees.

In a way, that made Clint unhappy. He had come out
here hoping to find a killer and now, it didn't seem that
this trip would be anything more than a pleasurable
visit.

"Come on inside." Lucy put her arm through Clint's
and escorted him toward the door.

"Anything I can help you with?" Earl Sturges asked,
glaring at Clint.

"No thank you," Lucy said. "It's been a long trip so
why don't you and the boys rest and get an early start
tomorrow morning."

"You want to come and see some good roping,
Gunsmith?"

"No thanks."

"I didn't think you would. You probably aren't up to
keeping pace with hard-riding, hard working men, are
you?"

"Earl! What is the matter with you?" Lucy said
angrily.

He realized he'd gone too far. "Sorry. Guess that the
funeral sorta put me in a mean frame of mind."

Lucy relaxed. "Mr. Adams is our guest. I won't have
him insulted, not even by our foreman."

The man flushed. "I'll take care of your horse."

"I'd prefer to do it myself," Clint said, not about to
leave Duke at this man's mercy.

"But . . ."

"Earl, you heard the Gunsmith. But thanks anyway."

Earl stomped away, back straight as a rod. Clint just bet that someone in the bunkhouse was going to catch hell this night.

"Don't mind him," Lucy said. "He gets that way sometimes. But he is the most loyal man I've ever seen. He'd give his life for my father."

"And for you," Clint said.

"Yes, I suppose." She watched Earl until he disappeared and it was hard to read her thoughts. Clint could not tell if she was troubled by Earl, comforted, or even flattered. But she knew how the man felt and that his outburst was due to jealousy. She had to know. Lucy Covington was a widow, not some naive girl.

"I'll show you where you can keep your horse, as soon as we've got you settled," Lucy said.

"Thank you." Clint followed her inside. He liked the way she moved. Lucy introduced him to Carmelita, her friend and their maid. The girl smiled shyly and bowed. "Señor Adams, welcome!"

Despite himself, Clint smiled back. He would find Ed Brisco's killer elsewhere, but for now, he figured he might as well enjoy the Covington hospitality.

TEN

The evening was beautiful and after dinner, Angus went to bed early, leaving Clint and Lucy to sit out on the veranda. They watched the stars twinkling brightly and listened to the sounds of men and families preparing for bed.

"My father loves this land," Lucy said quietly, "and so do I. But sometimes, I just want to go away and see something new. There's a whole lot of country beyond this tiny corner of Arizona. And I'll bet you've seen most of it, haven't you."

It was not a question. Lucy wanted him to tell her about other places and times. They were sitting close together on the porch swing and Clint rocked back and forth, content to enjoy the evening, the cognac in his hand and the girl at his side.

"Sure," he said. "I guess at one time or another, I've seen most of the West. Never been in the East too much, though. One time I went to North Carolina and there were so many trees that I couldn't see sunrise or sunset."

"You mean it's all forest?"

"Yep. The whole eastern seaboard is like that. It gives a big-country westerner a case of the jitters. A man can't see what's coming up on him in those forests. Everything is carved right out of them.''

Lucy shook her head. Being a desert girl, it was impossible to imagine. ''How do they run cattle or round up horses in that sort of country? Seems like they'd all get themselves lost.''

''They would,'' Clint answered. ''So they don't.''

''I sure wouldn't like that.'''

''I didn't, but it's all what a person is used to. Me, I like the beauty I've seen in all the western states. They're all different.''

''And the people?''

''Kind of the same. I mean, you can't look at a person and say, that fella, he's from Nevada and that one is from Montana. All you can be sure of is that there are good ones and bad everywhere.''

She studied him closely. ''And you've met your share of both kinds.''

''I have.''

''How many men have you killed?'' She took his hand and added quickly, ''I'm sorry, that's none of my business.''

''It's all right. I lost count on purpose. Too many, Lucy. Even one is way too many. But I never killed a man that didn't deserve to be killed, or that maybe tried to kill me first.''

''And women, I'll bet you've known your share of them too.''

''I've known a few,'' he admitted.

She chuckled. ''Don't try and fool me, Clint Adams. I can tell by looking at you that you have always attracted women. I'm even attracted to you.''

He was surprised at this bold admission though he'd guessed she might be. A woman just did not want to drag a man out into the moonlight to sit close and hold hands if she thought him pug-ugly. Still, Clint had always found that getting involved with someone who had a lot of money and power was sticky. They were accustomed to ruling over men, and Clint had never found that kind of thinking attractive.

"Clint?"

He looked at her closely. "Yeah?"

"What do you think of me?"

"I think you're a damn fine looking hunk of woman who probably is lonesome for a man. But I don't think I'm that man."

She reared back. Surprised. A little hurt and considerably angry. "And why not?"

"Because," he said easily, wanting to take the sting off his assessment. "You're a ranch girl and recently widowed. I think you're just sorta off-balance right at the moment and maybe a man who looks good isn't too good for you."

"Dammit!" she exclaimed. "I'm twenty-eight years old. I know my own mind."

"What about Earl?" he asked before he'd intended.

"What about him?"

"The man is crazy for you. He'll hate me if he finds out we were talking and sitting alone like this."

"So," she said, sliding away from him and speaking with contempt, "even you are afraid of Earl. Even the great and famous Gunsmith."

"I'm not afraid of the man," Clint said quietly. "I just don't need more trouble. Not until I find out who killed Ed."

"Then you'd better stay away from me or you might get hurt." But she was the one who was hurt.

Clint could see no choice: either he let her go in to bed alone thinking that he was a coward, or he take her into his arms, kiss her and let the cards fall where they might.

So he took her into his arms and kissed her hard. She made a small show of protesting at first, but then she melted and wrapped herself to him like a glove around his hand. Clint felt the heat rising in them both. "Maybe we ought to find us a bed inside," he breathed.

"We can't," she whispered, breasts heaving against her blouse. "If my father or Maria learned about it so soon after my husband's death, they'd think the less of me for it. I just can't disappoint them right now. Can't we go out to the barn and find a nice bed of straw?"

Clint grinned. "That'd be just fine. Lead the way?"

She took his hand and damned near jerked him off the swing she was so hungry to make love. Off the veranda and out across the moonlit yard towards the barn they raced. She was fast. Clint figured it was going to be one hell of a good time.

They got inside and she lit a small lantern and led them to a pile of new straw. Without a word, she began to pull off her dress and what he saw made his pulse quicken.

"Well, don't just stand there gawking!" she ordered with mock peevishness. "Get undressed, you grinning fool!"

Clint didn't need to be told twice. This was the kind of order he could take from a woman. Especially one who now stood in just her petticoats.

Clint unbuckled his gunbelt and laid it down. He kicked off his boots and then unbuttoned his shirt, then his pants. They had just fallen around his ankles when the barn door blasted open and Earl Sturges stood there with a shotgun in his fist and it was aimed right at Clint's belly.

"Get away from him!" Earl shouted wildly. "I won't let him abuse you like this, Lucy!"

She grabbed her blouse and covered her breasts. "Are you mad?" she cried. "Put that down."

"Not a chance," the big foreman said, advancing on Clint. "Your father will thank me from saving you from this worthless gunfighter. I know how to protect you."

Lucy threw herself in front of Clint and stood trembling. "You shoot, and you'll have to kill me! My father will never leave you this ranch. That's what you want, isn't it? The ranch!"

"And your love. Now step aside."

"No! I won't let you murder this man, Earl."

"He sweet-talked you into this, Lucy. He's no damn good!"

"Then neither am I because I wanted him more than he wanted me!"

The man began to tremble. He lunged and grabbed Lucy, then hurled her aside to stand before Clint. "I'm going to beat you to death with my fists, you bastard," he choked as he threw the shotgun into the straw, raised his big fists and charged.

Clint tried to grab his pants and pull them up from his ankles. There wasn't time. Earl Sturges landed a punch that almost knocked him through the wall. Clint fell trying to clear his head. A boot caught him under the jaw and sent him over backward. He heard Lucy scream and he knew that this was one fistfight he could damn sure not afford to lose.

Somehow, Clint rose to his feet and got his pants up. But things looked mighty bleak.

ELEVEN

Clint had no illusions about his fighting ability. He was good, maybe better than good, but not good enough to whip a man taller, heavier, stronger and younger than himself. All he had was an edge in experience and his own incredibly quick hands. That plus a cool, precise logic to throw up against Earl Sturges' wild fury.

"Are you sure you don't want to go on back to the bunkhouse?" he asked, as he finished buckling his pants around his waist and bought time to clear the cobwebs from his brain. It had been a long time since any man had hit him that hard. Clint spat blood and could feel loose teeth with his tongue. He knew with certainty that he would not be able to stand toe-to-toe with Sturges. He had no intention of doing that anyway.

"I'm going to tear your head off," Earl said. "I want Lucy to see who's the better man."

"I think she already has." Clint raised his fists but Lucy tried to push them down.

"Earl," she cried, "I swear I'll have Pa fire you tonight!"

"No you won't." Earl's handsome face broke into a smile. He had this all figured out. "What are you going to tell him? That you were fixin' to crawl into the

57

haystack with a goddamn stranger? You know what your father would think of you for that. Same as I do. I'm in love with you, but the first time you meet a stranger and get him alone, you act like . . . ."

Clint didn't want to hear another word. He lunged forward and his fist cut a clean arc that terminated squarely in the center of Earl's face. It was a beautiful punch, perfectly timed and it had all of his weight and strength behind it. Clint felt Earl's nose collapse under his knuckles.

The man staggered and roared in pain. He grabbed his busted nose and stared at his bloody hand. "I'm going to kill you," he said through clenched teeth.

Clint danced back. "Yeah, you already said you were going to take my head off. So come on and let's get this over with."

Earl charged. Clint tried to dodge sideways but he tripped over one of his damned boots and Earl landed on him. He saw one big fist looming and he twisted his face sideways but felt Earl's knuckles numb his cheek anyway. The man was on top of him and he was as strong as an animal. Clint tried to buck Earl off. Failed. He took another crunching blow and then kicked his legs up and locked them around Earl's ears and tore him over backward.

Clint staggered to his feet. He felt as if he had been run over by a freight wagon. Lucy was yelling for him to whip Earl, and dammit but he was sure trying. Earl charged again. Big, heavily muscled arms windmilling so hard and fast you could feel a breeze.

Clint waited until the last second, then he ducked and drove his fist into the man's kidneys as he charged past. Earl groaned and slammed into the barn wall. Before he could turn around, Clint clobbered him over the right ear. Earl staggered but did not fall. He twisted and sent a whistling right that connected and knocked Clint back a half step.

For a minute, they both stood panting for air, hearing their ears ring and Lucy in the background, no longer shouting but telling Clint he was winning. That he could beat Earl and that Earl needed a beating for the first time in his life.

"Sure he does," Clint wheezed, spitting blood, his torso battered and bare. "But next time, hire a professional brawler to do it!"

Earl came at him once more. He grabbed Clint and hurled him into a waist-high stall. Clint gagged as Earl grabbed his neck and bent him backwards over the stall. He felt as if his back was going to break if he didn't loosen the man's hold on his windpipe. Clint grabbed the man's wrists but they were like steel bands. Clint felt his back going so he drove his knee up and into Earl's testicles.

"Ahhhh!" the man bellowed, his mouth forming a big oval hole.

Clint filled that hole with his fist. His hand went numb with pain but he ignored it, and drove two powerful uppercuts. The first landed in Earl's solar plexus, and the second caught him as he was doubling over in pain and straightened him like a bent nail. Clint finished the man off with a thundering overhand right that knocked him out cold.

Lucy threw herself at him and he was too weak to stand. She was on top of him and kissing his battered mouth and she was crying too, telling him how proud she was of him. And to prove it, she rubbed her lush, bare breasts across his face and begged him to take her—now!

But just when he thought it was a prize well earned, a familiar voice roared, "What the hell is going on here!"

"Father!" Lucy leaped up grabbing for her clothes.

Clint managed to roll over and stare at Angus Covington whose face was blood-red and whose sixgun was pointed at his heart. Clint groaned. Some things, like making love with Lucy tonight, were just not meant to be.

Angus Covington was in his nightshirt and there were several of his men behind him trying to look into the barn. One of them bumped him and Angus swung around, furious that they should see his daughter like this. "Get back to the bunkhouse, all of you!" he shouted, firing his gun and sending a slug through the roof. The ranchhands vanished.

Clint stood up. He grabbed his shirt and pulled it on trying to think of something that would ease the tension and keep Angus from killing him on the spot.

Lucy saved him the trouble. "Father," she said, "I can explain everything. I lured Mr. Adams out here. It was . . . ."

Angus stepped forward and backhanded her across the face and when Clint took a step forward, the rancher cocked his gun and hissed, "Give me one more reason to pull this trigger. Just one!"

Clint froze. But he was seething inside and his words were hot. "Lucy is a woman. A free woman and you have no right to treat her like she was a child."

"Don't tell me how to treat my own daughter!"

Clint looked at the young woman whose eyes pleaded with him not to provoke her father further. And Clint should have taken the warning but he was right at the ragged edge. He'd been attacked and damn near whipped by a jealous and extremely powerful foreman, and now this pig-headed old tyrant was slapping his own daughter around and threatening to kill him.

"Lucy," he said, pulling on his boots and then

recklessly grabbing his gunbelt and buckling it around his waist. "I'll be in Broken Lance until I find out who killed Sheriff Brisco. You need a friend, someone to talk to, you come and see me."

Angus didn't like that piece of advice one damn bit. "She does, and I'll whip her to within an inch of her life!"

But Clint ignored him. He studied Lucy and she nodded, a smile forming on her lips that mouthed a silent "yes."

Clint turned his back on them and went to get Duke out of the stall. He saddled, mounted and rode out not looking at either Angus Covington or Earl Sturges, who was still face down in the straw, still out cold.

The Gunsmith touched spurs and Duke seemed eager to leave this ranch too. They galloped past the Mexican houses and down to the road. Clint turned north toward Broken Lance. He was hurting from the blows he'd taken by the stronger ranch foreman. But he ignored the pain by letting his anger burn it away.

As the miles passed, Clint cooled down enough to realize that old Angus Covington wasn't a bad man, not really. He was just far too possessive. And even that destructive characteristic was easy enough to understand when you took into account Angus had lost his wife and four sons. Lucy was all the rancher had left.

But Lucy was a woman and she was ready to leave this country. Until Angus Covington accepted that, not even Earl Sturges was going to be safe nosing around that beautiful young woman.

TWELVE

When Clint arrived late that night, Broken Lance was in an uproar. That very afternoon, a large Apache band had struck and burned out a ranch and then several small prospectors' camps south of town. Eight men and two women had been found punctured with arrows. There had been no survivors, but the tracks indicated that the Indians had moved southeast.

"It's a wonder you didn't run right across their path," the bartender said to Clint as he pushed a shot of his best whiskey across the polished mahogany bartop.

"They'd never have caught me anyhow," Clint said. "Not on that black gelding of mine."

"Can't never be too sure about that, Gunsmith. Sometimes, they get real cagey and run a white man into their trap. Sometimes they know shortcuts you'd never think would exist."

Clint nodded.

"Who'd you have a run-in with? Must have been one tough hombre."

"You'll know him if he walked through your door," Clint commented drily. He was unwilling to give a name. He had no intention of saying *anything* about what had happened at the Covington Ranch. There was trouble enough without starting that kind of gossip.

"Some of the boys here weren't too happy about your going out to the ranch with Angus and that bunch. They say you're going to side with the Covingtons against the prospectors."

"They can say whatever they want, but that don't make it so. I don't side with anyone. All I want is Ed Brisco's killer."

"You want him, I'll tell you who it was."

"Who?"

"Earl Sturges. You know why I'm sure of it?" The bartender leaned close. "Earl wants the Covington Ranch and Miss Covington for his wife."

"Not surprising," Clint said. "Anyone in their right mind wouldn't mind inheriting the ranch or the young lady."

"Yeah, but Sturges is the kind that would kill for it. You see, Ed Brisco was lining up with the prospectors. That meant that if he was successful, Angus would lose. If Angus loses, then so would Earl when he took over. It's that simple."

Clint poured himself another shot of whiskey. What this man was saying sort of tallied up the same way he'd been thinking. If Earl believed he was going to get the ranch, he'd fight and kill to protect it. But Clint worried that, if Earl had killed once, he'd kill again.

"Hey," the bartender said confidentially. "Don't say who told you."

"I won't."

"The Covingtons are powerful. They used to come in here and spend a lot of money. I figure they will again some day. Once this gold rush thing is over. You know?"

"Sure."

"Thanks," the bartender said, sounding relieved. "Sometimes, I forget it's better to keep your mouth shut and play dumb."

"That's a good thing to do all right." Clint downed his whiskey and paid for the bottle to take to his room. He was really hurting but it gave him some satisfaction that Earl Sturges would be hurting worse. That squashed nose of his was going to swell up like a rotten gourd.

He asked directions to Clair Morrison's place. He'd see her in the morning and ask a few questions. Clint walked out the door figuring he was getting closer to the truth. As he passed down the boardwalk, he saw a large group of heavily armed horsemen leaving town.

"Hey, Gunsmith! Come and help us kill a few murdering Apache!"

"Not tonight," Clint called back. "Maybe some other day."

They grumbled and rode out heading south. Clint shook his head. Riding with a mob like that was the last thing in the world he wanted to do. Those kind of greenhorns could get a man killed real quick. They were just the kind of quail a man like Geronimo would roast for his dinner.

THIRTEEN

Clint winced at his reflection in the mirror the next morning. He carefully shaved his bruised face and put on his best shirt and pants. He shined his boots because he had a hunch that a woman like Clair Morrison would be impressed by cleanliness. He sure hoped she had gotten a grip on herself by now. If there was one thing Clint could not handle, it was a woman's tears.

At the cafe, he noticed that everyone was nervous and short-tempered. All the talk was about the men who had formed a posse last night and went out to kill Apache. Last night, with a little whiskey, everyone had seemed to think it was a fine idea. But today, in the harsh light of morning, it was clear that these people were having some real second thoughts. Clint finished his breakfast quickly. He shared their concerns, but when someone asked him if he thought they ought to go out searching for last night's posse, Clint said no. He explained that two wrong moves don't make a right one. If anyone was going Apache hunting, it had better be the army.

Clint knocked on Clair Morrison's door at ten o'clock and she seemed pale, but collected.

"I have been expecting you, Mr. Gunsmith."

"Adams," he corrected. "But I'd sure prefer if you just called me Clint."

"Of course." She opened her door and led him into a small parlor, nicely furnished. It smelled of tobacco smoke and had a man's big easy chair. Clint knew at once this had been Ed Brisco's room, a place where he had found company in a good woman and a roomful of good books. When he sat down, he found his hand resting beside a fine briar pipe. He picked it up.

"I remember this pipe. It was Ed's. His favorite."

Clair Morrison nodded. Sniffled. "I want you to have it and enjoy it."

"I don't smoke pipes."

"You will this one, I'm sure," she said, coming over and taking it from his hands. She opened a humidor and filled the pipe with a particularly black and powerful smelling tobacco. "Here. I'll enjoy watching you smoke his pipe."

Clint figured he had no choice. He lit the pipe and inhaled. The smoke burnt his throat, singed the hair in his nostrils, made his lungs seize up like a clenched fist. His eyes stung and watered and he began to choke. He could see Clair through a watery film and she was smiling when she said sweetly, "You'll get used to it. Even Ed used to cough a little when he first lit that pipe up. But he loved it just as you will."

Clint pounded his chest and sucked in fresh air. He had forgotten Ed had favored a particularly powerful brand of tobacco from Arabia. By the taste of it, Clint figured it was about half ground up camel dung.

He cleared his senses and pretended to smoke the pipe without actually inhaling the damned thing. "Miss Morrison?"

"Clair, please."

"All right, Clair. Well, at the funeral, you were pretty upset and you did make some serious charges against Angus Covington. I wondered if you'd like to retract them, or if you have some basis of proof."

"Proof?" Her eyebrows arched imperiously. "What other proof do I possibly need? Angus publicly threatened to have our Ed killed if he didn't stop trying to support the prospectors."

Clint leaned forward. "He said he would kill him?"

"Yes. Right in front of the entire congregation one Sunday after church."

"I see." Clint frowned. "What were the circumstances?"

"They got into a terrible argument over land rights. Angus claiming he'd homesteaded the land in question while Ed tried to explain that he had no legal rights to it. That Angus had never filed a claim except to a few thousand acres he was entitled to keep by right of existing territorial law."

"I see." A threat made in anger, Clint knew, was not evidence at all. If it were, half the men out West would be in prison. Clint placed the stinking briar pipe down and said, "I'll leave this here for the next time I return."

"I hope that will be the day we both celebrate Angus Covington's hanging."

"Yes," Clint said, surprised at this woman's vehemence.

She showed him to the door and just as he reached the porch step, a cry sounded down the street. Clint heard gunshots and then saw four men from last night's posse come galloping in. They were whitefaced, two badly wounded and the other pair looked wild with fright.

"Geronimo is coming!" they screamed. "He's got a hundred men and he's coming to slaughter, burn and rape!"

A woman down the street screamed hysterically. Clint turned to look at Clair Morrison but she was already slamming the door and he heard the bolt snap shut.

Clint bounded off the steps and took off running. From the way people were racing for cover, it seemed Broken Lance was going crazy.

FOURTEEN

Because there was no law in Broken Lance since Sheriff Brisco's murder, Clint took over the responsibility for law and order. He forced open the sheriff's office and sent out word that anyone, women or children, who needed a safe place to stay while under attack could come and be protected in the jail. The walls were adobe, one foot thick and the ceiling was of Mexican tile. No flaming arrow could start a fire, no Apache could break down the doors.

Within ten minutes, there was a woman and about a half dozen of her excited children crawling around in the office. Clint quickly became annoyed at the screaming kids who kept running from window to window. He shooed them all into the twin cells and locked them inside with their mother. This was not a very popular move but he did it anyway—partly for their safety.

With the woman and her children shouting at him, Clint decided he might as well wait outside and maybe he could shoot a few Apache as they galloped down Main Street. There were plenty of other men with the same idea. Clint saw their faces and rifles peering anxiously through busted out windows. Geronimo was going to find that Broken Lance was a damn tough town

69

and that its citizens weren't about to roll over and play dead.

Time crawled by one second at a time. By noon, Clint heard occasional curses and he knew that the defenders were getting restless. Somewhere down the street in one of the saloons, an argument started and then Clint heard a table crash and two gunshots. Damn fools couldn't wait to kill Apache, they had to start on themselves first!

It was a hundred degrees in the shade by twelve-thirty and the woman and her six children locked in the cell were raising such a ruckus that Clint could not stand it a moment longer. So he grabbed a Winchester and marched down the street to the end of the town. Men in hiding called to him but he ignored them as he passed.

Clint looked out at the immense desert. He could see a hundred miles of surrounding country and, while he knew the Apache were legendary for finding cover where there wasn't any, Clint also knew that there wasn't a living soul out there. He did not doubt for a moment there had been Apache—those four wounded men sure hadn't shot themselves by mistake—but Geronimo or whichever bunch of Indians had ambushed them were much too smart to attack a town in broad daylight.

Clint turned on his heel and headed back through Broken Lance calling to everyone that there wasn't going to be any attack. At least, not during the daylight hours. People came out of cover with some reluctance and even some resentment. It was almost as if they were disappointed now that there was no immediate danger.

"You mean you kept us locked in this . . . this filthy cell for nothing!" one outraged mother shrieked. "Our little children locked in a cell for no good reason!"

"Well," Clint said, "you came here, I sure didn't drag you."

"This is outrageous!" the woman cried. "If you were our real sheriff I would start a petition to have you fired!"

Clint bit back his reply that would have informed the woman where she could have placed her precious petition. Instead, he forced an icy grin and said, "Yes, ma'am."

He watched them all hurry off, a cackling old mother hen who had probably driven her rooster into another territory.

The afternoon passed slowly and though men were stationed at both ends of the town, there was nothing to be seen of any Apache. Clint went to visit the four men who had spread the alarm. He found them fast on their way to getting drunk.

"You men had better slow down on that stuff," he advised, pouring himself a whiskey and taking a chair with them. "If the Apache come as you seem to be so sure they will, then we'll need your guns."

One of the men looked up at Clint. He had a long, hangdog expression and his eyes were glassy from pain and also from drink. "They killed eight of us last night," he said. "Came right out of the dark and got us."

"How?"

"I dunno."

"Me neither," said another survivor. "We was in rough country. Sorta got lost up in the canyons to the south of here. One fella, I think it was Arnie . . . ."

"Yeah, it was Arnie, all right."

"Well, he said, 'I know this here trail that'll take us through these canyons and make a loop that'll go back

to town.' So we argued about that for awhile and finished off the whiskey.''

"You were a bunch of fools to drink whiskey out
there in Apache country," Clint said, his eyes harden-
ing. "You're full grown men. You should have known
better.''

The first man nodded. "I know that now. We all four
of us do. But last night, it just seemed like we was in the
right. That we were doing something and we couldn't
fail.''

Clint shook his head. It would do no good to chastise
these men any more. They'd obviously suffered enough.
"So where did they hit you?''

"In a canyon. Goddamned if any of us knew where
we were. But the walls were all around us and it was
darker than the bottom of a well. All of a sudden, we
heard the twanging of bowstrings. Only we wasn't sure
it was that until someone screamed and shouted. He'd
been hit in the back with an arrow. Then the Apache
opened up from the rims. We all went crazy down there
in the dark. Started racin' back the way we'd come into
that damned old canyon. But they were expecting us.
Soon as we came out of the canyon into the moonlight,
they opened fire with their rifles.''

The man swallowed more whiskey and squeezed his
eyes shut. "It was awful, Gunsmith. We could hear
ourselves screaming, hear the sounds of horses going
down, bullets smackin' flesh. It was like they could see
in the dark. I never even looked back, not even when I
heard a man yellin' for help. I'm a damned coward.''

"We all four of us are, Bill.''

Clint relaxed. He laid his hand on the man's shoulder.
"Don't be too hard on yourselves, any of you. If you'd
stayed, you'd have died. There was nothing you could

do for the others. Running away was your only chance."

All four of them looked up at him, their expressions grateful. One spoke for them all when he said, "Hearing them words from a man as brave and famous as yourself, Gunsmith, well, that means a hell of a lot."

Clint tossed down his whiskey and took the bottle back to the bar. He came back to their table and said, "This town might be attacked by Apache yet. If it comes, it will be tonight. We need guards. I know you men were up all last night and I know what you have been through. But I sure would be grateful if you'd stay sober and help protect Broken Lance if an Indian attack comes before dawn."

To a man, they all rose unsteadily. Chins up, some pride back in their bloodshot eyes, they walked past Clint, each with a tight nod of his chin.

Clint watched them leave. They'd be out there tonight, and tomorrow, they'd be able to hold their heads up and look any man in the eye.

FIFTEEN

There had been no Apache attack that night, nor the next, but men did not forget their scalped friends and there was a lot of talk about another posse. Clint listened, amazed that men did not learn from hard lessons.

He spent the next few days going over Ed Brisco's papers, searching for some clues as to the murderer's identity. So far, he had no evidence. He did want to speak with Angus Covington again, though the last time they'd seen each other they'd parted under strained circumstances.

Angus saved him a long, hot ride when he and Lucy along with Earl Sturges and a heavily armed body of Covington cowboys rode into Broken Lance for supplies. Clint watched the men head for the saloon and he saw Angus and his daughter go into the general store to buy supplies. Earl posted himself outside the store. The big foreman crossed his muscular arms across his chest and appeared to be almost dozing in the shade, but Clint knew it was just a pose. The man was a rattlesnake coiled to strike.

Going across the street and facing either Angus or Earl wasn't Clint's idea of fun but he had come to find a murderer and he was eager to leave this hot country.

The sooner he meted out justice, the sooner he could ride north to escape the desert. So he checked his sixgun and dropped it lightly into his holster and tugged his Stetson down tight. He wasn't afraid of either man, and they were both the only real candidates he had for the murder of Ed Brisco. So if one of them was foolish enough to draw his gun, it was going to narrow the list of murder suspects by half.

Earl saw him coming before he was into the street. The Covington Ranch foreman dropped his hands to his sides and stood up straight. There was still a lot of swelling in his face, and his nose was purplish and crooked. Clint had no illusions as to how a man might hate someone for doing that to their appearance.

Earl stepped over to the edge of the sidewalk and said, "That's far enough."

Clint stopped. "Says who?"

"Me."

Clint just smiled and started forward until Earl casually added, "And the man up on the rooftop is about to blow your head off."

Earl might be bluffing, but if he was not . . . .

Clint stopped.

"Turn around and get your ass off the street," Earl said, the smiled transforming into a look of pure hatred.

"I want to talk to Angus before he leaves."

"He don't want to talk to you. And neither does Lucy."

Clint forced a grin. "I don't believe the part about Lucy. You see," he added with a reckless wink. "Lucy and I sorta hit it off. I might even come visit her real soon."

Earl got ugly. "You do that," he hissed. "It'll give me the reason I need to kill you."

"You already have the reason. You're so jealous that it's choking you to death."

"Why . . . ."

Whatever might have happened did not for one reason only, and that was that Lucy Covington spotted him through the window, understood instantly what was about to happen, and charged out between them.

"Clint!" she cried breathlessly, her face strained. "How nice to see you again!"

He spoke to Lucy, but his eyes never strayed from Earl's gunhand. "You too. I hope everything has settled down at your ranch."

"Oh, it has. It has! I'm glad I had the chance to see you again." She came over to him and slipped her arm through his. Tossing her head saucily, she glanced back at Earl and said, "Stay with my father, please. You know how many enemies he has in Broken Lance."

"Dammit, Lucy, you know your father told you to stay away from him!"

But Lucy ignored the man and they walked off down the street just as easy as you please. Clint thought that any moment he might get a bullet in the back but it never came. He could feel the sweat of fear trickling down his spine.

"Don't worry, he won't kill you."

"Are you sure?"

"No."

"Thanks," Clint said. "Mind telling me why you risked my life just now?"

"I had to talk to you."

"I'm listening."

"I think Earl killed Sheriff Brisco."

Clint did not lose stride. "What makes you say that?"

"Who else would stand to gain so much if we were married?"

"You'd consider marrying him?"

"I was until I laid eyes on you."

Clint shrugged. "Your interest in me isn't much good for my health, Lucy."

She laughed softly. "I want to finish what we started in the barn. Can you come out to the ranch?"

"Will your father order me shot on sight?"

"No. I'm going to convince him that Earl murdered the Sheriff, or had him murdered. Ed Brisco and father were very close."

"You don't have a shred of evidence, do you?"

"No. Do you?"

Clint shook his head. "Not yet. Most people think Earl is the man I want, but suspicions don't make the man guilty."

"I have a young man on the payroll. His name is Chet. He's madly in love with me. I allow him that privilege," she said with a smile to show she was only teasing. "I'm going to ask Chet to keep his ear to the ground and try and get something on Earl. I'll also use him to send you messages. The moment I have anything, I'll send him. He can be trusted. I'll point him out to you as we leave."

"All right."

She reached up quickly and kissed him on the mouth, right in front of the whole town. Great, Clint thought, Earl will hear about that and it'll be one more nail in my coffin.

"I'll see you soon, darling."

She hurried away to disappear inside a millinery shop. Clint shook his head. That girl was going to get him into a pile of trouble before this was all over with, but if she was as delicious as she looked, she was worth it. Besides, maybe she was the only one that could possibly help him unravel the murder of Ed Brisco. True to her word, Lucy signalled to Clint as she and her father drove out of town. Chet was very skinny with brown eyes and light brown hair.

That evening, Clint played a little faro and won twenty-three dollars. But the betting was light. Most of the prospectors had abandoned their claims and come into town until the threat of Indians was past. Clint gathered up his poker chips about ten o'clock and headed for the hotel and a good night's sleep. He decided that, if he did not hear from Lucy within two days, he was going out to the Covington Ranch and confront both Angus and Earl Sturges with his suspicions.

He was crossing the street when a rifle's boom filled the corridor of buildings. Clint felt the sting of a bullet across his ribs. He threw himself down and rolled, his gun coming up in one smooth, incredibly fast motion. He saw a shadow between the buildings and fired as quick as thought. The sound of his gun and that of the rifle melded in one long blast. Clint rolled once, fired again and heard a cry of pain. The dark form vanished.

People crowded cautiously around the doors and windows of the saloons to see who had gotten killed this time. Clint ignored them as he leapt to his feet and took off after the man. He rushed into the alley and then his warning senses told him to hit the dirt. He did just as a rifleman opened fire at the end of this tunnel of darkness. Clint saw the stabs of flame and fired right into them. He heard a body strike a wall and then there was a deathly silence.

Clint struck a match and walked over to the man.

He was finished. Clint grabbed the body by the ankle

as his match died. He turned around and dragged the man out into the street where the light from a saloon revealed his ambusher's face.

"Anybody know who this man is?" he demanded, expecting it to be a Covington gunhand.

"Well, sonofabitch," a prospector whispered. "That's Roy Beyers!"

"Who the hell is he?"

The prospector scratched his head and looked at Clint. "I'm ashamed to tell you this, but he's one of us!"

Clint dropped the man's leg and walked away with a feeling of disgust. None of this figured at all. Maybe Earl had hired Roy. Maybe not. One thing sure. Someone was trying to kill him and prospector or not, Earl still topped the list of candidates.

SIXTEEN

The next day Clint asked a lot of questions and received damn few answers. Roy Beyers had been a loner, like most prospecting men. There was only one thing about Beyers that was at all interesting. He had money. A bank account in each of Broken Lance's two banks. Neither bank, however, would reveal the amount, except to say that Beyers had apparently been a married man for he'd left a will stating that the money was to be sent to a Mrs. Nellie Beyers of Wichita, Kansas.

Clint spent several difficult hours that afternoon penning a long letter to the lady explaining that he had killed Roy Beyers in self-defense and that he would see the man was buried properly. It did not escape Clint that he was spending a lot of money on tombstones and caskets these days. He also told Mrs. Beyers that he was happy that she was going to be well taken care of and that he hoped she might write back immediately and tell him if she had any idea why her husband had tried to kill him.

That evening Chet appeared out of an alleyway as Clint passed. "Got a message from Lucy," he said.

"She wants to see you."

"When and where?"

"Beside that spring in the meadow you pass on the way to the ranch. The one just three miles from the ranch. Midnight."

"Tonight?"

Chet nodded. Although he was an awkward young man, with an overlarge mouth and slightly buckteeth, there was strength in his jaw. His brown eyes were steady and unwavering. Clint had the impression that, given another few years, Chet would grow into his height and be a pretty fine hunk of manhood. Whenever Clint had seen him around Lucy, the young man was so worshipful that he would have done handstands if Lucy asked, or fetched sticks. Anything to please or amuse her.

"I don't like you," Chet blurted. "You might as well know the truth of it straight out and honest."

"All right. I appreciate a man who says what's on his mind. Thanks."

Chet blinked. "Whadda you thankin' me for? I just said I didn't like you and I thought maybe you might kill me on the spot for that—not thank me."

Clint laughed quietly. "I never killed a man yet for being honest with me. How you feel about me doesn't matter a whit, Chet."

"It will if you hurt Lucy." Chet thumbed back his hat. "Mister, that girl has already lost one husband and been hurt enough."

"And you're going to protect her?"

"Yep."

"Then I'd suggest the one you really ought to worry about is your foreman, Earl Sturges."

"He's been warned too."

"Then why is Earl letting you stay on the payroll?"

" 'Cause I'm the best bronc-buster and wild horse

catcher in the whole damned Arizona Territory. There ain't nobody I ever seen could rope or ride the way I can."

Chet might be awkward and shy about Lucy, but he sure wasn't modest about his own cowboying abilities. Clint just shrugged. "Well, thanks for the message —and the warning."

"You ain't welcome," Chet said, but he said it without any heat before striding off into the darkness.

Clint shook his head. At least, he reasoned, he didn't have to worry about Chet ambushing him. That boy was straight-up honest.

The air was cooling and the stars were sprinkled liberally across the heavens. Duke had not been out of his stall in several days and it seemed like a fine night to go for a long ride.

Maybe, Clint thought, Lucy has some important news. Some bit of information that would finally shed light on the puzzle of Ed's death. Clint hoped so. He was ready to leave Broken Lance and if these people took his advice, they'd give all this country right back to the Apache.

He met Lucy Covington just after midnight and they tied their horses up in a nearby draw, then walked over to the spring where Clint drank deeply. "Why is it that desert water is always sweetest?" he asked.

She shrugged her shoulders and moved sensually over to where the grass was highest. He could see her clearly in the moonlight, a tall, winsome young woman with a smile on her face as she began to undress for him.

"Pleasure before business?" he asked. "I came because I hoped you had some information for me."

"I do, but it can wait. Like I've been waiting for you."

She was completely undressed now and he whistled softly because she was a real beauty. Long, clean lines but a deep chest that told him she had a lot of heart and desire. Clint pitched his hat down on the grass, then unbuckled his gunbelt while she unbuttoned his shirt down to his navel. She bent and let her tongue flick at his nipples and he felt himself shiver.

"You're pretty hungry, aren't you Lucy?"

"I haven't had a man in a good long while," she said huskily. "And I hope you're in as big a hurry as I am."

When she had his shirt off and then began to pull down his pants, she laughed. "I guess you are very hungry. And ready enough to satisfy the most greedy or shameless woman!"

He took her into his arms and kissed her roughly, sensing she wanted him to be that way with her the first time. This was to be urgent; a violent joining of eager bodies. He welcomed that. So he pushed her down onto her back and pulled her legs apart. His hand went down to discover she was already wet and he played with her womanhood, rubbed it with the tip of his finger until she began to writhe with pleasure in the grass.

"Oh, Clint," she begged, "please don't play with me. Do it now. Come into me!"

"All right," he grunted, plunging his huge staff into her all the way to the hilt and then rotating his hips into her hard.

"Ohhh!"

Clint started to pull back thinking he'd given her too much too fast.

She reached up and grabbed his buttocks. "No, don't

pull back. Give me all of you!"

Clint smiled in the moonlight and was only too happy to follow her orders to the letter. He began to piston in and out until the wet, sucking sound of their union filled his ears and drowned out her moans. He felt her hands gripping him tightly and pulling his body into hers all the way.

"Yes, yes," she groaned, "oh, I'd forgotten how it could feel so good. I . . . ."

She never finished her sentence. A cry filled her throat and then she began bucking wildly and scratching his back with her nails. Clint didn't mind. He liked a woman who forgot herself and went crazy under him.

His own body responded powerfully and he drove in and out of her in long, thrusting strokes until he lost control too. His hot seed filled her and they rolled over and over in the warm, sweet grass.

Later, he asked, "Before you work me to death, Lucy, why don't you tell me what you found out about my friend Ed's death?"

"Not much," she admitted. "Only that he was grubstaking a miner or two on our range."

"Are you sure?"

"Yes. My father told me that. It was the reason he figured that Ed and he were on opposite sides of the fence and there was no getting back together. Sheriff Brisco had money riding on the side of the prospectors."

Clint sat up. "Damn," he whispered. "It's hard to believe. Ed must have changed a little."

Lucy kissed his cheek. "Ed was a fine man. He did nothing wrong. To his mind, and to the minds of all those prospectors, much of the range my father claims is free land. You can't blame any of them.''

"And what do you say, Lucy?''

"I don't know.'' She tried to smile. "I just know I'm my father's daughter, right or wrong. And I'll stick with him, no matter what.''

Clint took her back into his arms and kissed her tenderly. Of course she'd side with her own father. But she was torn by it. Anyone could see that she was. And without saying it straight out, Clint had the hunch that Lucy would give this damned old land back to the Apache too, given a way out. But as long as her father was here, she'd stay and fight.

Clint admired her and figured that, if he had a father—even one as ornery and bullheaded as old Angus—he'd do the very same thing.

SEVENTEEN

The next afternoon, Clint went to see Clair Morrison again. As soon as they were seated in her parlor, he asked, "I've been informed that Ed was grubstaking some of the prospectors. Did he ever tell you that?"

The woman blinked with surprise. "Who told you such a thing?!"

"Never mind. I just want to know if it's true or not."

Clair fidgeted nervously. "You know, Ed and I might have got married and gone away if we'd have had any money. On the salary they were paying Ed he couldn't hardly support himself, much less a wife. I told him that he had to start looking after himself a little too. Not always just the town. He was getting on in years, you know."

"It happens to us all. And you were right. Ed wasn't in this business for the money. So he grubstaked a few miners. Is that it? How?"

She stared at her hands. "There are ways a lawman can earn a dollar here and there. Ways that hurt no one."

"I'm sure not about to play judge or jury. Who did Ed stake?"

"I don't know."

"It's mighty important that you tell me, Clair. It would help me find out who killed Ed."

The old woman's eyes flashed. "I already told you! It was Angus Covington or his foreman, that awful Earl Sturges. They killed Ed!"

"I can't prove that," Clint argued, picking up his hat and starting for the door. "Maybe if I knew the men Ed grubstaked, I'd have something more to go on."

He stopped at the door and peered back into the gloomy house. The woman was sitting in a chair, her body bent and yet very stiff. "Mrs. Morrison, I know you hate the Covingtons, but don't let that hate stand in the way of us finding out the truth. If someone else killed Ed, we want to see him get sentenced to prison or the gallows. Don't we?"

She nodded. "Yes." Her voice was as brittle as October's fallen sycamore leaves. "Yes!"

Sometime late that night, Clint heard his door splinter from its hinges. He rolled and grabbed his sixgun just as two men crashed into his room.

"Freeze!" he shouted, swinging the gun on them. "Or you're dead!"

Standing silhouetted against the hall lamplight, Earl looked huge and forbidding. Beside him, equally as tall but very thin and nervous stood Chet. Both had their guns pointed at the Gunsmith, both wore expressions that said they were mad enough to die foolishly. Their eyes swept the room. Chet dropped to his knees and peered under the bed.

"Where is she!" Earl snapped.

"Who?"

"Lucy, of course. What'd you do with her?"

Clint shook his head. "I went to bed alone. She's

never been in this room. Maybe you'd both better put those guns away before we get ourselves killed. Then you can tell me what this is all about."

"Jesus Christ," Chet choked. "The Apache musta got her! That's the only explanation for any of this!"

A chill went through Clint. When Earl and Chet started to spin and leave, he fired his sixgun into the doorway over their heads. "Hold it!" he yelled, hopping out of bed. "Just hold it or I'll shoot you both in the legs before you take a step out of this room!"

They knew the Gunsmith wasn't bluffing. They turned and Earl said, "She came to see you tonight."

"Why!" Clint demanded.

Chet looked miserable. "I don't know. She had some fool idea and there was something about the sheriff's death she wanted to talk to you about. I thought I'd convinced her not to come here alone. Not with Geronimo and his Apache raiding hereabouts. But after we went to bed last evening, I thought I heard a horse galloping out on the desert. I couldn't be sure. Finally, I got to fretting about the Indians, thinking maybe they were sneaking up on the ranch. I went outside and checked the horses. That's when I saw that Miss Covington's horse was gone."

Clint set his gun down on top of the bed. He grabbed his clothes and started pulling them on fast. "Did you tell her father?"

"Hell no!" Earl shouted. "We figured she was coming to see you and we wanted to protect her good name. Chet woke me up and we both been riding like bats outta hell ever since."

Clint shook his head. "Did you come across any Indian pony tracks out there?"

"Yeah," Earl said, his voice dropping in defeat.

"They crossed Miss Covington's and we lost them but they were heading for Old Mexico. Chet and I were hoping that she'd missed them Apache by a few hours."

Clint finished dressing. "Not very damn likely, is it?"

For the first time, Earl spoke without hatred. "So what are we going to do to get her back? The nearest U.S. Army post is nearly . . . ."

Clint buckled on this gunbelt. "You know what would happen if we tried to get the army in this. Lucy would be killed for sure. Got any money with you?"

The question caught the two men by surprise. "A little, but . . . ."

"A little won't do it," Clint said roughly. "We need a hell of a lot of cash and we need it fast. The only hope to get Lucy back alive is to find Geronimo's band and then buy her freedom."

"Couldn't we sneak into their camp and steal her away?" Chet asked hopefully.

"Not a chance," Clint replied. "Does Angus have much cash at the ranch?"

Earl glanced at Chet, then said, "He keeps a can of greenbacks hidden somewhere in the house. Enough to handle any emergency."

"This is an emergency," Clint said tersely. "I'll need cash and I'll need it in a hurry."

"You're not coming!" Earl snarled.

"Try and stop me," Clint said. "That girl was coming here to help me. I feel responsible. And one more thing, her only chance is if I go alone. A bunch of men would just invite ambush or else cause Geronimo to run farther and faster than he already will."

Chet stepped back into the room. "I got a stallion that'll outrun and outlast anything alive. I'm comin' with you."

"I'll ride the stallion," Earl growled. "He belongs to the ranch. You ride the second best horse. You're light and you can get more out of it anyway."

Clint frowned. On the one hand, he didn't want any help, but on the other, he had to think not of his own preferences but instead concern himself with what was the best for Lucy. A man alone stood damn little chance down in Mexico chasing Apache. He couldn't stay awake day and night, nor could he hope to stand off even the weakest attack. But three men, heavily armed and willing to fight to the death was another proposition entirely.

"All right," Clint said. "You can come along. But if Angus tries to join in, or to send any more men, then we split the blanket. I won't lead an army of greenhorns on Geronimo's trail."

Earl nodded. "You got it figured right about the small numbers but I'm going to be the one in charge, not you."

"We'll see about that," Clint said, stepping forward and raising his fists. He had whipped this big, obstinate s.o.b. once, he could do it again right now.

"Wait a minute!" Chet shouted. "The last damn thing we need is to fight among ourselves. Kill each other after we rescue Miss Covington if you want. But not now!"

Clint hesitated. He lowered his fists and Earl did the same. They both knew that the skinny kid was right. No matter how much they disliked each other, they had to stick together and work together. Their lives and Lucy Covington's depended on nothing less.

Clint holstered his gun and stuffed his clothes into a big canvas warbag. Satisfied that he had everything he needed, he picked up his rifle and headed out the door.

"We'll get all the food we need from Angus."

"He won't like not going after his daughter."

"Of course he won't," Clint said impatiently. "But he's smart enough to know he'd soon be slowing us down. He'll also know that any more than three men will be a death sentence for Lucy."

Earl sneered. "You think you've got it all figured out, don't you? Well, you haven't because what you don't understand is that Mr. Covington might just decide to have you shot and send one of my chosen gunmen in your place."

Clint nodded. "I thought of that too," he said, pushing into the hallway and heading for the stairs. "I'll just have to take that chance."

Earl cursed but Clint didn't bother to even look back as he shouted. "Better get at least five thousand dollars to bring along. With that much money, we can raise an army of Mexicans if we need to attack Geronimo."

Earl cussed again, but he didn't argue any more.

He needed to marry Lucy if he was to get the Covington Ranch. Funny, Clint thought, three men on the trail to Mexico and all for slightly different but vital reasons. With Chet it was puppy love. Earl wanted the ranch, the power and the money, and I want to save a girl who tried to help me find Ed Brisco's murderer.

It was going to be a damned interesting ride south.

EIGHTEEN

Lucy Covington was frightened nearly half to death. She knew that she had taken a chance in going out alone to see Clint, and yet it had seemed so very important that she'd gone anyway. But when she'd gone no more than five miles, she had come across three riders who quickly fanned out and came after her.

At first it had been a good, exciting chase. Lucy prided herself on her horsemanship, and the mare she rode had racing blood in its hot veins. Lucy had been widening the gap between herself and her pursuers when she realized that she had been turned east and was being chased toward a wild, empty country. Country that her father claimed, but never used because it was so dry and hostile. It was filled with box-canyons, deep barrancas, and the rare water holes known only to the Apache and the few renegades that traded guns, horses, ammunition, and slaves with them. The three who followed her were such men. She knew because they traveled this country which ordinary men would never approach. Usually Anglo, but sometimes half-breeds or pure Mexicans, these traders had to be more vicious and cunning than the Apache themselves. They were men who would sell their own sisters and even mothers if there were a

92

few dollars to be gained in profit.

Lucy had seen a few of these men, mostly hanging by her father's rope or else attracting buzzards. Angus called them "breathing carrion." He ordered them shot on sight. But now they were driving her deeper and deeper into the wastelands toward New Mexico.

Dawn was just an hour ahead. Lucy twisted in her saddle and studied the riders for perhaps the thousandth time. They were a little farther back, but still coming. Dark, lean outlines atop black devil horses that could not run as fast as her mare but might run farther.

Lucy bent down and adjusted her weight in the saddle for her mare's benefit. The animal was laboring already, she had used it too hard. The horse was stumbling, its breath sounded like overworked bellows in its deep chest.

"I'm sorry," she said to the mare as she pulled it down from a slow gallop into a trot. The trot was very uncomfortable but Chet had once explained that it was the easiest way for a horse to travel fast over very long distances. "I pushed you too hard. We have to pace ourselves!"

She let the mare trot for five minutes which seemed like forever, then she glanced over her shoulder to see that the three men had also slackened the pace and were similarly trotting their horses.

Lucy had not expected that. She had thought they would keep at the gallop and that she would turn and find them much closer but that their horses would not be so fresh as her own. A miscalculation. Even worse, her own mare was not refreshed. The animal was still breathing hard, still covered with foam and showing every indication of weakening.

Lucy pulled the mare down to a walk. She pleaded

silently for her horse to catch its breath, to renew its swiftness and strength. She waited another five minutes and this time when she turned around in the saddle, her breath drew in sharply.

They had not slowed to a matching walk but had stayed at the trot. The "breathing carrion" were several hundred yards closer. Within the rifle range of a marksman. But they would not shoot her. Lucy knew that she was worth a great deal alive. And if they recognized her as the daughter of Angus Covington, she would be worth even more to them.

The mare stumbled. Lucy had to yank hard on the reins to get the animal's head up or it would have gone completely down. The mare was a showy, Sunday kind of a horse. A horse bred to race on a smooth dirt track, a horse more used to bluegrass, oats and a curry comb than to cactus and rocks. Lucy glanced around again. The mounts those men rode would be ugly and thin. They would be considered runts and culls. And they would run her mare into the ground over forty miles of this kind of desert.

I have to turn back soon, she thought. Every mile I go diminishes my chances of finding help, or having someone come and save me from these animals on my trail. Lucy's hand dropped to the wet and trembling coat of the mare she rode. "Just keep ahead of them until noon tomorrow," she begged. "By then, we'll be back on home range and my father's men will see us. They will kill them. We'll be home again by tomorrow afternoon. And I'll never do anything this stupid again!"

NINETEEN

Mid-morning found her crossing into New Mexico Territory, a land as desolate and lonesome as any she had ever seen. Three times in the last three hours she had tried to turn back toward the Covington Ranch. Three times they had expertly moved into a position which forced her to ride farther east. Even worse, each time she had whipped the mare into a desperate break for freedom, the animal had responded more sluggishly. It had no speed remaining. No heart to go on. A front hoof was split up the middle. The mare was starting to limp. When the men behind her saw this, they would close in for their catch.

Lucy wiped the sweat and dust from her face with her sleeve. Her lips were cracked, her cheeks raw with the heat and the wind-blown grit she had faced before dawn. Her canteen was low, her spirits even lower. But someone would know she was missing by now. Her father would be riding after her with men. Enough men to save her from whatever awaited.

Lucy cursed herself again for not taking the time to bring a Winchester rifle from the house. But then, that would have been a dead giveaway if someone had seen her crossing to the barn. She did have a pistol stuffed in her riding skirt pocket. She knew how to use it if she had to. And it looked as though she would definitely have to.

The mare stumbled over a rock and fell. Lucy stayed in the saddle and pulled it back to its feet. The mare barely made it. The game was almost over. Lucy had been expecting it for hours. Her sleek, bay racing mare was dying on its feet. Its sides were heaving in and out and it wasn't sweating at all anymore. It did not take an expert horseman like Chet to know that the mare needed water and rest or it would not live until the end of this day.

Maybe, Lucy thought, neither will I.

She angrily chided herself for that thought. She would fight and she would live. To go back to the ranch and tell her father that she no longer wanted to live in this awful country. That she wanted to see some color and life, some beauty. Pines, lakes, green, green grass. The world had those things, her eyes yearned to see them all. Was that so wrong?

Will they rape me? Probably. And if they try, can I kill myself first? Probably not.

Tears flowed down her cheeks. She looked back. The breathing carrion were within pistol range. If she used the sixgun in her skirt pocket, she would lose her advantage of surprise. They would wait until she emptied the gun and then they would take her as easily as if she were a baby.

Lucy pulled the dying mare to a standstill and dismounted. Her hand slipped inside her skirt pocket and she waited. All around her the mountains were a pale lavender. The sky was a soft blue and the sun had no more mercy to it than the men who followed.

She turned to face the pursuers. Behind her, the mare nudged her as if asking to be forgiven. Lucy reached back and stroked its muzzle. "You did the best that you could do," she whispered. "I'm sorry."

At a hundred feet, the riders reined their runty little horses to a standstill. They were Anglos, but she knew that by their sharp facial features rather than the dark, teak-wood color of their skin.

They dismounted. A matched trio of breathing, stinking carrion. She saw a smile cross their lips as they realized she was young and pretty, even though she now felt very ugly and very old. They started forward.

Lucy drew herself up tall. "Stop right there!" she ordered. Surprisingly, they did. "My father is Angus Covington. I know that you've heard of him. He owns a big ranch. He has a lot of money and I am his only child. He will pay you to take me home."

They looked at each other—and laughed even louder.

Lucy backed up next to her dying horse. She had never been so afraid. Their laughter was an obscenity that bounced off the surrounding hills and bled into nothingness.

They came for her and she slipped her hand into her skirt and gripped the small, .36 caliber Colt pistol. She wondered if her skirt would catch on fire when she fired through the material at them. She didn't care. If she burned alive they at least would not be able to use her like some coyote bitch in the brush during her time of heat.

"That's far enough," she choked when they were close enough to smell. They began to laugh again and when one of them reached for her, Lucy raised the barrel of her gun and shot him right in the stomach.

The man's laughter died on his lips and his face reflected shock and then pain. He dropped and as Lucy tried to tear the Colt out of her pocket, the other two men lunged for her. Lucy felt her skirt burning. She went down with them on top of her. She felt their clawing and tearing at her and then the world of pain consumed her like a fire.

She knew nothing more.

TWENTY

Angus Covington was like a man possessed but Clint didn't care. He stayed on Duke and let the old rancher rave and screech until the man grew hoarse and silent.

"You want to go on Geronimo's trail with a big pack of men, you go right ahead," Clint said. "But I think you've got more sense than that. Three men might have a chance to buy your daughter's freedom. Any more than that will be an open invitation to kill hostages."

Angus didn't like to admit that Clint was right so he said, "I hold you responsible for her, Gunsmith. It was you she was riding off to see."

"That's right. And it was you who made her sneak out in the night."

Angus Covington's face flushed red, but Clint did not care. He was fed up with this entire situation and wished he'd just gone on alone to search for Lucy. But it was far too late for wishing, and it would be dawn in less than one hour.

The ranchyard was filled with cowboys. They stood silently in the shadows and moonlight, smoking quietly, trying to beat down their anger at not being able to ride out and hunt the kidnapping, raping, murdering Apache down.

Clint saw Chet come out of the house with two

bulging saddlebags. It was the ransom money. Earl had fresh horses saddled, the stallion and another that looked like it could run like hell. They also brought another animal and it was packed with supplies.

Clint frowned. "The pack horse is going to have to keep up. I won't be slowed down by it."

Earl finished tightening the straps and cinch. "The pack horse is carrying the least weight of all. He'll keep up. Besides the money, we brought some trading goods along with a big surprise."

"Be specific."

"Guns and ammunition," Earl said. "Things far more valuable to the Apache than money."

Clint didn't like the idea of putting good weapons and ammunition into the hands of the Apache. But what Earl said was true. It was also true that, should they get trapped somewhere and placed under siege, the guns and ammunition would prove mighty valuable. "What's the surprise?"

"Box of dynamite," Chet said. "My idea. Could come in real handy."

"Could get us killed, too," Clint reasoned, though he thought it was worth the risk.

He looked to the old rancher. "We'll find Lucy and bring her back if she's alive."

Angus Covington nodded. "Either way, alive or dead, this is her home and I want her here. Earl! Chet! I don't care if you have to carry her body a thousand miles to get it home and buried beside her mother. This is where she belongs, you understand me!"

"Yes sir!" they called.

"Good. You boys bring her back and you'll be rewarded—but fail—fail and this country ain't big enough that we won't find you."

"Let's ride," Clint said turning Duke south and

touching his heels to the animal's flanks. They were already a good six or seven hours behind the Apache who had taken Lucy. It was a long distance to make up in this kind of country.

They came across the tracks one hour after dawn.

Clint stepped out of the saddle and studied them closely. He walked all around the scarred meeting ground until he was sure that he had all the information he was going to get from the signs.

"Well, goddammit!" Earl said with heated impatience. "You're just gonna tell us what we already know, ain't you! And we just wasted five minutes watching you play Apache tracker."

Clint thumbed back his Stetson. "Lucy came along a good two hours after the band of Apache had already passed."

The two men stared at him in disbelief. "If that's the case," Chet asked, skeptically, "then why'd she turn east and follow the Indian ponies?"

"She didn't. Not on purpose, anyway." Clint remounted and stared across the miles of heat-beaten land toward New Mexico. "My guess is that she was traveling fast in the dark and never even saw the Indian tracks. She turned east because someone else made her do it."

"What!"

Clint felt his anger rise to the flash point. "Listen, both of you! I'll be damned if I'm going to argue everytime I learn something. You don't believe me? Fine! Follow the Apache ponies to hell for all I care. But I'm telling you, she was running free when she came here and something made her veer to the east."

Clint said no more. He set Duke into a ground-crunching canter that took him east and brought him to a place where the tracks of three other horses merged and then covered those of Lucy's mare.

"You can read the signs for yourselves now," he said, moving on and letting the two reach their own conclusions.

"Who the hell are they?" Chet demanded as he caught up to gallop stirrup to stirrup with Clint.

"I don't have any idea. But they must not be friendly or Lucy would not have run from them in a direction she did not want to go."

"Sonofabitch!" Earl whispered. "If we can overtake them before they reach more Apache, we might just finish this up before tonight."

"Maybe they never even caught up with her," Chet said hopefully. "You know how fast that mare of hers is, Earl."

"Yeah," he said, but did not sound very hopeful.

"And we both know that she ain't made to run this kind of country."

"But. . . ."

"Just shut the hell up!" Earl snapped. "If they caught her, it'll be a mean thing and I don't even want to talk about it until it happens. Understand?"

Chet nodded stiffly. Clint knew the kid was hurt and angry, but grudgingly admitted Earl was right. Some things were best left unsaid and unthought. Before the day was out, they'd know if Lucy had gotten away or not. But three to one were long odds and if Clint were a betting man, he'd not bet on Lucy Covington. Not against the kind of men you'd find ranging country like this. They were the kind who'd not hesitate one damn moment to shoot Lucy's running horse right out from between her pretty legs.

TWENTY-ONE

"Please," she begged, "don't kill my mare! Father and our men will find her and take her home. The split hoof will mend."

In answer, Rufus sent a bullet into the mare's brain. Lucy threw herself at him and raked his face viciously before Wade sent his fist crashing against her jaw. She dropped and tasted blood in her mouth.

"Get up!" Wade hissed, grabbing her by the arm and dragging her to her feet.

The one whose face she had raked balled up his dirty fist and would have broken her nose except that the one who held her spun her out of his reach. "Rufus, we ain't going to get a damn thing for her if you beat her to death!"

Rufus lowered his fist. He was of average height, but with very wide shoulders. His arms seemed much too long for his torso and one of his ears was bitten half off.

"How much is your daddy worth?"

Lucy shook her head to clear her mind. "A lot," she said trying to think straight. "He's rich."

Wade grabbed her face and squeezed it between his thumb and forefinger. "You ain't lying to us, are you?"

"Look at me! Do I look poor?" Lucy demanded.

"All right, let go of her!" Rufus hissed. "Let's make us some money!"

"How we gonna do that without getting ourselves killed?"

"I don't know. Maybe the lady here has an idea or two."

Lucy tried to think clearly. She knew that these were cautious men, men used to tricks and treachery. They would not appreciate a suggestion that would put them into any obvious danger. "One of you could ride back and meet whoever is following. Tell them they'll have to pay you if they want to see me again."

Wade spat into the dirt. "Let's sell her to an Apache chief down in Mexico. A woman with blonde hair and white skin will bring a hundred dollars easy."

"My father will gladly pay you ten thousand dollars!" Lucy cried. "That's more money than most men hope to earn in their entire lives! Are you so afraid to take a chance?"

The pair studied each other in silence. Lucy could almost hear their twisted, fried little brains weighing the odds.

Wade made his decision. "I say this. Only a fool would ride back into Arizona and meet up with whoever will be following. They'll hang him for sure."

"Not if they really believe you will kill her if I don't return by a certain time," Rufus said. "A rich man, he wouldn't think nothing of handing over the money for his daughter."

"We don't even know for sure her father is rich!"

"Look at the damn mare she was riding!" Rufus shouted. "Look at the way she was dressed. And look at that saddle, bridle and blanket. That's money! It's all the best you can buy."

He reached down and pitched Lucy's dress to her.

"Get yourself covered up or you'll blister in this sun, lady. Put your hat back on too."

Lucy did as she was told. She had been used but instead of destroying her, their assaults had only heightened her resolve to see them dead. Lucy had never known hate so strong. Hatred would carry her through anything that lay ahead. She had listened and watched the man she had shot in the belly die, and he had not died well. But if necessary, she would die bravely. Like a Covington, with courage and dignity.

"You want to go back there, you go then," Wade shouted. "I think you're a fool. A hundred dollars for the woman, another fifty for her saddle and outfit. Her gun is worth twenty dollars, easy. That's not bad money. Even split two ways it ain't."

But Rufus wasn't listening. "I got a feeling," he said. "I got this feelin' that this is our lucky day. That this lady is going to make us rich before we are finished with her."

"Rich? How about dead?"

"No." Rufus shook his head. "I gotta try this. You stay right here. See that last ridge of mountains we crossed?"

"Yeah." The ridge was a good twenty miles away.

"If I got the money then I'll flash this piece of mirror at the sun when I come over it. That means everything is fine. But if you see horses coming and no mirror flashin', then it means I was wrong to go back. You know, our usual signal."

Rufus walked over to his horse and swung into the saddle. "If I'm wrong, you know where to go and how much money to ask. I'd say that Chief Caddo is the most likely to pay best for a woman like that. He's too proud to show good sense and pass on a woman that looks like that. You tell him she shot Arnie in the belly. That'll raise her worth even more in his eyes.''

Wade nodded. He looked over at Arnie's body. "We pull this off, it'll be better just the two us anyway.''

"Not for you it won't be.''

"What the hell does that mean?''

Rufus looked down from his horse. "Means I'm the one taking all the chances on this deal. I get two shares, you one.''

"No, goddammit!''

Rufus smiled. "Does that mean that you want to ride back instead and let me stay here with the woman?'' He actually started to dismount.

"All right! One third is still thirty-three hundred dollars. Don't let them talk you down, now.''

"I won't. She said ten thousand, that's how much it will be. You make camp over yonder in the shade of that rock. Keep the horses out of sight.''

"Won't do no good.''

"Why not?''

Wade glanced over at the bodies of the man and the dead mare. "Buzzards will start to circlin' within an hour or two.''

"Then cover 'em with dirt and rocks and stay closer. That'll help some.''

Rufus turned his horse around and started back west. Lucy watched him go, wishing he were staying instead of Wade. But it didn't really matter, she would have to kill whichever one stayed.

TWENTY-TWO

Clint saw the rider coming across the long stretch of desert. The man seemed to be in no hurry.

"What do you think?" Earl asked. "Is it one of them?"

"Don't see who else it would be," Clint answered. "Looks like he's tied a white flag to his rifle barrel and wants to talk."

"I'll kill him," Earl hissed.

Clint turned on the ranch foreman. "You do that, and we'll never see Lucy alive again. And if that happens, I'll kill you. It's that damn simple, Earl."

For a long moment, their eyes locked. Then, Earl glanced away but when he spoke, his voice shook with anger. "When this is over and Miss Covington is safe, you and me are gonna have a showdown that only one of us is going to walk away from."

"Suits me right down to the ground," Clint said. "Meanwhile, you just keep a lid on that temper of yours and let's see how much money this maggot thinks he can get out of us."

Chet angrily sleeved his face of sweat. "I wouldn't pay them a single red cent!"

"I'll pay them what it takes. Once we have Lucy, we

can go after the money. But Lucy is the important thing.''

"At least we agree on that much," Earl rumbled. "But remember what I said about after."

Clint ignored the big fool. If there was to be a show-down between them, let it come later. Right now, all his attention was focusing on the rider coming toward them. And he was enough to attract any man's complete attention.

He was about six-foot tall, rangy and with a full, black beard. He wore a slouch hat that was pulled down low over his forehead. His clothes were a combination of Apache leather leggings and bright red scarves around the neck coupled with a castoff, army officer's blue tunic. The tunic was crusted with grease and dirt. It still had a few of its gold buttons but the shoulder epaulettes were missing both the braid and most of the fringe. He was armed to the teeth. Clint counted three pistols and one big double-barreled shotgun that he had cradled in the crook of his left arm. He rode an Indian saddle which was little more than a couple of pads under a square of leather with two dangling stirrup straps made of braided horsehair. The stirrups themselves were broken wooden things bound together with wire.

The horse he rode was a dun, but one so crusted with dirt and sweat that its color might have been mouse-brown. It was skinny but its head was up and bobbing and the animal seemed excited.

"Jesus, will you look at him." Earl whispered. "What is he?"

"Renegade trader," Chet said.

"I know that! But I never seen one that looked so damn raunchy."

Chet, the horseman, was looking at the stranger's

mount. He just shook his head in wonder. "That little mustang he's riding couldn't weigh much over six hundred pounds. But look at him throwing his head and prancin' thataway!"

Clint said, "Why don't you both stay back while I talk to him? Might make things a little easier."

"Not a chance." Earl punched the steel to his stallion's ribs and the animal jumped forward.

"That's far enough, boys," the man said, yanking hard on the reins of his mustang and managing to point his shotgun in their general direction. "As you can see, I am carrying the flag of truce."

"Tied to a gun barrel," Clint called out.

"Odds are in your favor, boys. But we got the girl. She tells us that her daddy is a very rich man."

"Not so rich," Clint replied.

The renegade white man laughed. "To men like ourselves, even ten thousand dollars is very rich! Eh?"

"We didn't bring anything near that amount, damn you!" Earl shouted.

The renegade stopped smiling. "Mister, you had better watch your manners. First one to die if this party goes nasty will be you."

Clint figured the man was wrong. But there was no way for him to know that he was facing a real gunfighter. "We have five thousand dollars to play with," Clint said, jerking a thumb toward the saddlebags. "Bring us the girl and it is yours."

The man laughed softly. "Don't work that way, friend. You pay me now, then we send the girl back to you."

"Like hell!" Earl shouted. "You don't get any money until we have her back."

The rider simply shrugged his shoulders and lifted his

reins to turn back. "I will consider the matter with my partners and let you know our decision."

"Don't move!" Earl shouted reaching for his gun. "You ain't going anywhere!"

The stranger lifted the shotgun and would have blown a hole in Earl big enough for pigeons to have flown through. But Clint saw the first move and his hand streaked for his sixgun. He drew and fired, aiming for the man's shoulder to wound instead of to kill. But the excited mustang was spinning around and Clint's bullet went through the man's lung. Even then he might have lived long enough to tell them something of value except that Earl's gun was bucking in his fist. The stranger was knocked out of the saddle, only one of his feet hung up in the stirrups and he went bouncing alongside his horse as it raced away.

Clint was furious. "Well, we did it now! Chet, go catch that little horse before it runs itself to death out here. If he's got a canteen, bring it along—and search him carefully."

Chet looked at Earl. "He givin' the orders now?"

"Do as he says," Earl replied, reloading his gun and savagely jamming it into his holster. Chet took off.

They topped a ridge and looked across a great distance. At first, Clint saw nothing, but then he noticed the buzzards floating way up in the sky. They were little more than black specks but they were circling.

They waited until Chet managed to get a rope over the mustang and cut the renegade down to search him. When Chet came galloping up to rejoin them, Clint started Duke down the long ridge saying, "You find anything?"

Chet shook his head. "Nothing but a few gold pieces and a bag of pesos."

Suddenly, from miles away, they saw a bright glint of sunlight. It danced off something and winked like a star. Once. Then twice. Three times. Clint twisted around in the saddle. "It's a signal! Did the dead man have a mirror, piece of shiny metal. Anything like that!"

"Yeah but. . . ."

Clint swung Duke around and raced back to the body. He found a broken piece of mirror in the man's tunic pocket and galloped back to join Chet and Earl. Clint flashed the mirror so that it could be seen across the great distance that separated them from Lucy Covington and the men who held her captive.

He could raise no answering signal. Clint swallowed his crushing disappointment. Maybe there had been a signal that he could not have duplicated by guessing. But maybe not. All he knew for sure was that something had been prearranged and that the men ahead now understood that all deals were off.

Clint wondered if that meant that they killed Lucy, or just that they would race ahead on better rested horses.

He hurled the mirror at a rock and it shattered into a hundred pieces. Clint didn't care. He was racing off the long ridge and into the desert wasteland.

TWENTY-THREE

Wade swore violently and knew that something was very, very wrong. The signal from Rufus should have come much sooner. And when it finally did come, it was all jittery. Not like they had used so many times before. Two flashes, then you cover the mirror with your hand. Then two more flashes.

"Rufus is dead," Wade muttered to himself. "That's the only way they could have got the damn piece of mirror offa him. He's dead!"

Wade's big fist closed on the mirror and broke it. He cut and bled but didn't feel anything as he turned to face the woman. Rufus and he had ridden together for five years and saved each other's lives more times than he cared to remember. Rufus had been a second cousin. He was mighty smart too, but greedy. Always greedy and trying to milk the last dollar out of the Apache or squeeze a peso until it screamed. Well, greed had made him lose his good sense and it had cost the fool his life. Too bad. He had been a good partner. Dangerous as a badger when cornered, honest as a man who dealt with slaves and Apache could be, but just too damn greedy.

Wade studied the woman. "Rufus bought it and I ought to kill you since you're the cause of this."

Lucy backed up a step. She had slipped a rock into her pocket and was waiting for one unguarded moment to try and bash this man in the skull. All she needed to do was stun him for one second and then she could grab a gun and finish him off. She had never expected she would kill anyone, but then neither had she dreamed of the nightmare she was caught up in now. And at this very moment, the man was coming toward her with murder in his eyes.

"Stay away from me," she said in a trembling voice as her hand strayed into her pocket and closed on the rock. "Stay away!"

He slapped her in the face and she tried to pull the rock out and hit him but he knocked it out of her hand and hurled her across their camp. "Get mounted up, damn you! Put your good saddle on Arnie's horse and hurry up or I'll shoot you in the belly and leave you ascreamin' in the dirt!"

The very thought of that sent her to her feet and racing for the horse. He would kill her now if she gave him the slightest provocation. But they were coming. Her father, Earl and how many others she did not know. From this distance, she couldn't tell. But they were on this animal's trail and closing. By tonight, she told herself. By tonight they will overtake us and I'll be safe.

She deliberately slowed her work until he shouted at her and raised his fist to strike. "Aw, get outta my way!" he bellowed, shoving her aside and tearing her saddle off the dead mare to throw on Arnie's horse. "Grab up the canteens and come on!"

"Where? Don't you see that your only hope is to take both these horses and relay them to safety?" She hadn't meant to make that suggestion. The thought of him escaping revolted her and yet, she knew that if it came down to him escaping or her living, she would choose life. "I'll tell them to let you go!"

"The hell you will!" He grabbed her by the hair and hurled her up into the saddle. "Make one false move, try to escape, signal, do any damn thing at all and you are a dead lady."

She nodded dumbly. He took her reins and sprang onto his horse. They lit out at a fast trot. The horse she was riding was so rough that it took all her effort just to keep from being battered nearly to death. Where were they going?

South! He was racing straight south towards Mexico now. Did the fool really think that her father and Earl would respect the border? No, he was not that stupid. Lucy gripped the saddlehorn. He was going to find his Apache friends. The ones that he and his two dead partners had traded with. That they would trade her to. What was the chief's name that they had mentioned? Caddo? Yes, who was he? Did it matter?

Lucy glanced over her shoulder at those who followed. She could barely see a thin line of dust on the far horizon. It would be night soon. Her father was not a tracker and neither was Earl. She tried to think of one single person on their payroll who was an expert tracker. There were none. She hung onto the saddlehorn and prayed for deliverance.

They found Lucy's mare and the body of the renegade she had shot and they all took a measure of grim satisfaction in knowing that Lucy had made them pay a price. There had been three before, now, there was only one.

"So what is the man's destination?" Earl asked.

The Gunsmith didn't hesitate. "Mexico. Deep into

Mexico. He'll trade Lucy to an Apache for gold.''

"Geronimo?''

Clint shrugged. "I don't know. All I'm sure of is that we have to rest the horses for an hour. And by then, it will be dark and it will be slow going if the ground gets any rockier.''

"Then let's go on now!'' Earl raged. "Use the light to close the distance.''

"No,'' Chet interrupted. "The Gunsmith is right. These horses are about played out. We can't keep pushing them so hard. The pack horse is about done in.''

"Then we leave it!'' Earl stormed. "All three of us are still riding strong animals.''

"No,'' Clint said. "Lucy is a good fifteen or twenty miles ahead. Their horses are rested and all we'd do is kill our own if we run them another night.''

"So we let him get away!''

Clint took his canteen and poured a little water into his hat for Duke to drink. "No,'' he said without looking up at the big man, "we start using our heads instead of our feelings. We start thinking about finding more water and how we are going to overtake and rescue Lucy. It's going to be a few days. It won't happen tomorrow.''

"The hell with that!'' Earl raged. "I'm leaving now!''

Clint pulled his sixgun and the sound of it cocking brought the foreman around. "You came to play a hand in this game. I didn't want you along but you came anyway. Now, I'm telling you one last time that you are going to play this by *my* rules. We stick together and protect each other or you go back the way you came. Right now. Same goes for you, Chet. We got to have one man in charge and I'm appointing myself.''

They didn't like it one damn bit. But they'd already seen Clint draw and shoot and even Earl knew his life had been saved by the Gunsmith. And neither one of them were worth a damn as trackers. They'd lose the trail before midnight and wind up riding dozens of aimless miles searching for Lucy's tracks in the morning.

They needed the Gunsmith, and he knew that was the only reason they hadn't gotten together and turned on him for the kill.

TWENTY-FOUR

Three days had passed and Clint knew that they had lost any chance of overtaking Lucy and her captor. Not only did the man have a huge lead, but also he knew where water was to be found and that gave him a tremendous advantage.

Now, almost a hundred miles into Mexico, the desert grew even more harsh. The heat intensified until it was impossible to ride during midday. And they were low on water again. Clint had only drunk a small cupful in the last thirty-six hours, preferring to give his share to Duke. It hurt the Gunsmith deeply to see the big black gelding endure so much suffering.

"We need to find a waterhole real soon," Chet said in the raspy, dry voice that comes with thirst. "These horses are dying on their feet."

Clint nodded. "I know that. There has to be water just up ahead somewhere. The man we follow wouldn't ride any deeper into this country unless he knew where to find it."

"We're falling behind them more every day," Earl complained. "They're going to just vanish in this goddamn country and we'll never see her again. We can't go back without her, Chet. You heard Mr. Covington."

Chet barely nodded. If Earl wanted some show of support or encouragement, he was out of luck. Clint had quickly noticed how this grueling ride had altered Chet's opinion of Earl Sturges; the kid barely acknowledged the man as his foreman anymore. Clint had anticipated this. Earl had just not seemed like the kind of man who endured suffering gracefully.

Clint stopped and rose in his stirrups to point. "Those low mountains," he said. "I think they angled toward them. Maybe for water."

"That's what you said the last time," Earl growled. "I think we ought to keep riding straight down this valley. You know they didn't climb the mountains on either side. We can pick up their tracks and gain a couple of hours."

Clint said nothing. He was tired of arguing. He just reined Duke toward the mountains waiting to see what would happen.

"Hey!" Earl bellowed. "Godammit, Chet! Get back here. You take orders from me, not him!"

Clint twisted around in his saddle and saw that the kid was following. Despite himself, Clint smiled, feeling his lip crack and sting. Chet had switched loyalties and now Clint knew things were going to go a whole lot smoother. It was still two going to be two against one, but Earl was now the one.

They climbed into the low mountains, but the going was very slow because the ground was littered with shale and loose rock. Tracking was difficult but the longer they continued following the trail, the more certain Clint was that they would find water. Water was the only reason anyone would come up here.

Two miles up, they did find water. Duke's ears pricked forward and his step quickened. They passed around a small scree of boulders and there it was. But Clint's heart sank because the small spring and precious water was fouled by human and horse excrement.

"Sonofabitch!" Earl screamed. "I'll kill him!"

Clint dismounted and handed Duke's reins to Chet. He gritted his teeth and swept the excrement away with his boot. He then took off his belt and used his buckle to start digging a catch-basin into the rocky ground where fresh water would seep. The basin would hold nearly a pint of water.

"It will take about an hour to fill up each time. We'll be here until tomorrow morning letting the horses have their fill and then filling up our canteens and our own bellies. Might as well get down, gents, and get comfortable."

Earl shook with fury but his tongue licked at his own cracked lips and he dismounted. Clint watched the spring slowly wet the powdery dirt in his catch-basin and turn it dark. So damned slow.

His eyes strained south and he thought of Lucy out there somewhere. They'd have been in and out of this waterhole in two or three hours. One thing for sure, the man he was following knew his business. He was hard and ruthless and desert-savvy.

We'll never catch him until he gets where he's taking Lucy, Clint thought. And that's all there is to it.

TWENTY-FIVE

Lucy knew they were at the end of the trail. She could see the Indian camp just ahead. It blended in with land and she would not have even noticed it had it not been for the oasis of meadow that always meant water. She could smell the meat cooking and now she saw a few horses being watched by a boy. As she came nearer, she saw the crude brush shacks and lean-tos used by the Apache as shelters from the sun. Now, she saw the Indians themselves as they rose to their feet and came forward with rifles.

Lucy felt her stomach knot up and her heart began to pound with fright. She looked to the hated white man beside her and almost pleaded for his protection. Then she realized how foolish it was to expect anything from him—he was going to trade or sell her as a white slave. He would let her go to the highest bidder who would defile her and treat her worse than a dog.

Lucy felt her eyes sting. She would not cry, not in front of these people. They despised weakness and she was not weak, only hopeless. She did not blame her father or their men for not being able to overtake and rescue her. She'd seen how Wade had used the rocks to hide their trail and cruelly fouled every water hole.

"You don't say a damned word or I'll stuff my

knuckles down your throat," Wade hissed. "You smile and look friendly."

"Go to hell," she told him, tossing her head defiantly.

He would have backhanded her off the horse as he had done several times already but a group of Apache children bolted out of the brush into their path and startled their horses. Wade nearly lost his seat and had to grab mane to keep from spilling into the dirt.

He was furious at almost being unseated. A few of the children giggled at him but he ignored them, fixing all his attention on the men who waited in grim silence. As soon as they were in the center of the camp, Wade pulled to a standstill. He dismounted and, with a broad smile on his face, he began talking in Apache. The words were unintelligible to Lucy. There were as much grunts as words, short, guttural in nature.

Lucy had intended to keep her eyes on a far mountain range and show no interest in these people. But now that she was among them, she couldn't help but look at them closely. She had only seen dead Apache before. Angus had let her see a few of them. But alive, they looked very different. They were not handsome people, but she had not expected them to be. They were short, squat, powerful with square faces and bad teeth. But despite that, Lucy also saw something she had not expected. The young mothers looked at her without hostility, the girls were openly admiring and a little shy. The boys stood with wide, staring eyes. Children of both sexes under five were wearing only a breechcloth, their skins were very dark, their eyes as black as their hair.

Lucy concentrated all her attention on the littlest children and ignored the angry taunting of some of the toothless old squaws. She decided that children were forever children. There was really very little difference between them up to the ages of five or six.

Their camp was a terrible place, thick with flies, a few barking dogs, charred bones of a dead horse. Lucy tried not to think about the Covington Ranch headquarters. Her home, her own comfortable room with its nice furniture and the cool adobe walls to protect her from the summer heat and from all danger and hardship. She now realized just how blessed she had been all her life. But for God or chance, she might have been born one of these Apache destined to suffer so much harsh deprivation.

"Just stay on your horse," Wade ordered, glancing nervously up at her. "Don't do or say anything."

Lucy had no intention of doing or saying anything. She watched the children until a small group of the tribe's leaders came forward. Now, she watched the white slave trader as he began to talk even more rapidly. He used his body, hands and arms to gesticulate and emphasize his points. She could tell he was explaining how she had killed Arnie because he pretended to pull a gun out of his pocket and push it into one of the Apache's bellies. The leaders studied her much more closely now. Lucy shivered under their hard scrutiny.

Listening to Wade's high-pitched and very rushed wheedling, Lucy realized that the man was almost as afraid as she was only he hid it better.

The talk went on and on and the day seemed to get hotter. Lucy clung to the horse with her knees. She felt the sun driving its heat through her Stetson and cooking her brain. The hills began to shimmer and then the world seemed to take a slow roll and spin. Lucy grabbed for the horse she rode but missed.

The next thing she knew, she was lying in a brush shade and staring up at the flat, inscrutable face of an old Apache woman. The woman held a gourd of water and when Lucy tried to grab it, the woman pulled it away and pinched her cheek very hard.

Lucy cried out as much in surprise as pain and anger. She grabbed the woman's wrist and twisted it with all of her strength. The squaw flailed at her but Lucy was too strong and she pushed the woman over backward and tottered to her feet. She started to move towards the brush but a warrior stepped into her path and grabbed her with an iron fist. Lucy reached up to rake his eyes but something in them told her she would die if she followed through with her intentions. She lowered her hand and willed herself to be still.

The warrior's face was only inches from her own.

He was fierce-looking and his eyes made her feel like a mouse looking into the unforgiving face of a gopher snake. Taller than the average Apache, he smelled of sweat, horse and smoke. His body rippled with muscle and she knew better than to struggle.

He released her and when she did not try to run, he took her hand, yanked her to his side and then pounded his chest. "Caddo!" he proclaimed. "Me Caddo!"

He touched her on the shoulder and said, "You, me!"

Lucy stared up at him feeling her heart break. The meaning was crystal clear. He had purchased her for his squaw. She looked over to the campfire and saw Wade sitting crosslegged beside the dead fire.

He was chewing on a bone, all bent over like a ravished animal. But he seemed to feel her eyes on him and he looked in her direction. Then, he winked and she saw his body rock with mirth.

He was laughing! Lucy raised her head. She was going to live if for no other reason than to see him pay for this with his life.

TWENTY-SIX

Clint dismounted and crawled to the top of a low rise of land. He bellied down on hot rock and shaded his eyes while Earl and Chet did the same. For a long time the three men were silent and then Earl grunted with disgust, "I told you we wouldn't see nothing out there!"

He started to rise but Clint grabbed his arm and held him down for a moment longer. "I think I did see something," he whispered. "Way out there near those mountains it looks to me like a patch of green."

"In this desert!"

"That's right," Clint said stubbornly. "The Apache know where to find water and we're not so far from the Rio Escondido. It flows not more than twenty or thirty miles west of here."

Earl was not impressed. "Twenty or thirty miles of desert. Besides, I thought you said you didn't know much about this land."

"I don't. But I once knew someone who lived down here and she told me a few things about this country. The Rio Magdelena is about eighty miles on over that mountain range. I might stop by and visit it if we clean up this business and get Lucy safely across the border."

124

"Do that," Earl said. " 'Cause you shore ain't welcome back on the Covington Ranch."

Clint moved back down the hill toward the horses with Chet matching him stride for stride. "What do we do next?"

"We wait until dark and ride over and see what we can. I think the Apache might light a small fire to guide us by."

"But what if the bastard who's got Miss Covington kept on going? Maybe she isn't even there. They were three days ahead of us, Clint!"

The Gunsmith stopped and faced the young man. He had grown to like and trust Chet. The kid was dedicated and smart. He was without guile, a quality that Earl Sturges possessed enough of for ten men. "Listen, I hate to tell you this, but I don't know any more what might happen out there than you or Earl. All we can do is sneak up on the camp and see how things go. If Lucy is there, we might get lucky and see her. Maybe even try to sneak into the camp just before dawn and rescue her."

"Into an Apache camp?" Chet made it real plain that he thought the idea was suicidal.

"What would you suggest? That we go in with blazing guns? How much of a chance would you give Lucy if we did something that stupid?"

Clint laid a hand on the young man's shoulder. "I know you want her out of there real bad. So do I. But we can't go off half cocked. We have to pick the right time. If the slave trader is there, he'll speak Apache and tell them we are enemies. Apache killers looking for scalp money. I don't speak Apache. Do you or Earl?"

Chet shook his head.

"That's what I figured," Clint said. "If they are just

ahead, we have to go into this with our eyes wide open and our brains working, not just our trigger fingers. You follow what I'm saying?"

The kid nodded and looked up the hill at Earl. "Yeah, but I make no promises about him."

Clint understood perfectly. "All I can say is that Earl doesn't want to die anymore than we do. I'm counting on that fact to make sure he uses his head when the time comes."

"And if you're wrong?"

"Then I figure we're soon going to be in a whole lot worse shape than Lucy Covington."

They rode out just after dusk, moving in single file so that they were less likely to be seen until it was completely dark. There was a three-quarter moon and that was good and bad. Good because it would allow them to at least see shapes in the camp—and Lucy's shape would be immediately recognizable—bad because they could be seen if they needed to run.

It was funny, but Clint thought again of Juanita Sanchez. How she'd looked and felt. She was entirely different from Lucy Covington but they were both a lot of woman when it came to making love or war. But if he had to give the odds of either of them still being alive, those odds would be pitifully small. Neither Lucy nor Juanita were the kind that made good slave material. They'd probably rather fight to the death than submit to a life of grinding hardship and humiliation. Apache squaws were known to torture white slaves, and the tortures were almost as bad as those used by their men.

"Look!" Chet whispered.

Clint pulled Duke to a standstill. The Apache had lit a

small campfire for cooking. One minute it was just a
dark place in the land, the next it glowed very faintly
because the Apache were too wily to allow the actual
flames to be seen. They'd probably dug a pit and what
Clint was seeing was the sparks rising like a swarm of
fireflies.

"What would you say?" Earl asked. "Two miles?"

"That's pretty close. I think we can ride another mile
before we get off and move in closer on foot."

"If I see her, I'm going in there for her," Earl said
grimly. "I ain't going to let some buck. . . ."

"Why don't we decide what to do when the time
comes instead of wasting time talking about something
that might not be too smart?"

Before Earl could reply, Clint moved Duke forward
into the night. The animal was extremely weary, and yet
walked with its head up and eyes picking the best trail
through the cactus and brush. Clint heard a rattlesnake's ominous warning but before he even thought to
rein the gelding out of danger, Duke veered sharply and
chose a safe path. There were not many horses that were
as trail savvy as the black gelding. On a good horse, a
man could go right far.

When he judged he'd ridden a mile and less than one
to go, Clint dismounted and left Duke ground-tied. The
animal would stay put until he returned. Chet and Earl
tied their mounts and all three men quietly slipped their
rifles out of their saddle scabbards and moved forward.

There was a dry wash that ran towards the camp and
they used it to advance at a crouch. Clint kept his head
low and moved very carefully. They dropped to their
bellies and began to crawl the last hundred yards.

They did not see the warrior squatting in the wash

doing his private business until they almost bumped into him. The man was so surprised he had trouble getting his breeches up.

But his mongrel dog had much quicker reactions. It was big and hungry looking and came at Clint with a growl low in its throat. Not wanting to fire and alert the entire camp, Clint swung his rifle at the dog and caught it in midair as it went for his throat. The mongrel's growl turned to a yelp as its body struck Clint and knocked him sideways.

The Apache shouted a warning. He had no weapons, but that didn't stop him from attacking with the same ferocity as the dog. Clint tried to regain his balance and get his rifle up to club the Apache, but Earl couldn't wait and he didn't use his brains. Instead of silencing the onrushing Indian with a blow, he shot the man in the chest with his Winchester. Then, the fool shot the mongrel as well.

All hell broke loose not fifty yards from where they stood in the wash. Clint knew they had no chance at all of rescuing Lucy now. If they tried to rush the camp and grab her, they'd be slaughtered.

He wanted to kill Earl worse than the screeching Apache! The man had ruined everything. "Back to the horses!" he shouted. "It's the only chance we have left!"

Chet and Earl didn't argue or blink twice. They knew their chances of getting out of this mess alive were slim or none. Chet shot up the wash like a man born to run. His long legs and his youth carried him out ahead of Clint and Earl who ran side by side, laboring in the heavy sand.

Clint wanted to tell the man beside him that he was going to kill him the first chance he had. But that de-

pended on reaching Duke and getting some space between himself and the Apache.

This was the biggest mess he had ever found himself
in—and probably the most hopeless. Maybe it served
him right for bringing along a hot-headed, murdering
fool.

Clint sucked in all the air his lungs could take. He
lowered his head trying to ignore the shouting and now
the gunfire behind him. He lifted his knees and pumped
his arms as best he could carrying a rifle in one fist.
Slowly but surely, he inched away from Earl who was
already breathing like an overworked steam engine.

The man cried out, "Wait for me, Gunsmith! Don't
leave me behind!"

But Clint did not ease up one damned bit.

TWENTY-SEVEN

Somehow, they did reach their horses, all of them. But the Apache were right on their tails and were mounted on fresh ponies. Clint untied the pack horse, then grabbed his own saddlehorn and swung onto Duke. He did not need to spur the big horse because it knew what was required. And though worn down and in need of both food and water, the black gelding responded valiantly. It shot out of the wash and thundered across the desert as if the hounds of hell were on its heels. Clint had to hold the animal in or the packhorse would not have been able to keep up.

Earl and Chet were also well mounted and they followed closely, letting Clint and Duke pick out the best path of escape. Each time Clint twisted around he could see the Apache fanned out behind them. They were falling back, but Clint knew the Indians would just keep on their trail even if it took fifty miles to overtake their quarry. The Apache were a very patient people. They knew that only fools rushed themselves or their horses in the heat of the desert, and then they paid dearly for their folly.

Clint heard a shout and turned around just in time to see Chet's horse somersault and toss the cowboy into the brush. Clint reined Duke in hard.

He circled back around to Chet and shouted, "Jump on!"

But the cowboy was knocked out cold. Clint looked up to see the Apache bearing down on him. They had seen Chet's horse fall and they knew that their first victim was as good as dead.

Clint jumped off Duke and ran to the cowboy. Chet was alive. There was a nasty gash on the side of his head, but it was nothing that would kill him if he were given the chance to live. Clint meant to give the kid a fighting chance. There was a large jumble of rocks less than two miles away. If they could reach it, maybe there was yet some chance for survival. He snatched up Chet's canteen, then yanked his Winchester free and grabbed the young man. It was a good thing that Chet only weighed about 150 pounds soaking wet.

"Leave him, goddammit!" Earl shouted. "Come on, he's finished."

Clint didn't even bother to answer. A man had to live with his own conscience and Clint had never done anything so shameful as leave a man helpless to be tortured then scalped. He would not start now. Besides, if Chet could be revived, they'd need his gunhand if they stood any chance of fighting off the Apache. Clint had no illusions about outrunning the Indians on his trail. If they had been on fresh horses, well-fed and well-watered, sure, but that just wasn't the case anymore. Even an animal like Duke had his limits, and reaching those rocks ahead of the Apache would test them to the fullest.

He threw Chet over his own saddle. Then, because there was no time to tie the kid down securely, Clint swung up behind the cantle of his saddle and sent Duke running toward the big pile of boulders.

Duke ran with all his heart, but carrying double and

given his weakened condition, the big horse was losing distance to the Apache with every labored stride.

A bullet whistled past Clint's ear and he drew his gun. It was no easy trick trying to hold Chet across the saddle, rein Duke, and then turn and fire over his shoulder off a racing horse. For one of the first times in years, Clint missed his shot. He swore silently to himself, then tried again and his second bullet scored. The nearest Apache who had been steadily closing now flipped over backward and landed rolling.

The others set up a yipping ruckus but when Clint turned around again to take the next man out, the Apache had fallen back twenty or thirty more yards, just far enough to be out of effective handgun range.

Clint holstered his gun and yelled, "The rocks! We'll make a stand in the rocks!"

Earl cussed violently and slowed his horse until it was running side by side with Duke. "Gunsmith! Throw Chet off and let's make a real horserace out of this!"

"No," Clint shouted. "We have no choice but to make a stand and fight. Besides, what about Lucy? Are you going to toss her life away too? She's all the future you've got, Earl. Think about that!"

Earl did think about it. He knew he was licked.

Alone out here, he would have no chance at all of reaching the United States border and the safety somewhere miles beyond. If the Apache behind them didn't run him down, some more of them up ahead sure would. Reluctantly, the burly foreman set a new direction toward the rocks. But he sure didn't hang back to protect Clint's backside. No question about it, the man was one hundred percent for himself.

Earl reached the protection of the boulders about five seconds ahead of Clint. The man shot through a narrow gap and jumped off his horse yelling, "Come on!"

Clint could feel Duke giving everything he had left in that final quarter of a mile. The Gunsmith let the big horse set his own maximum pace and when it carried them into the safety of the boulders, he stepped out of the saddle, pulling Chet with him. The first thing he did after laying the kid down behind a rock out of harm's way was to grab Duke and pull him back deeper into cover. Then, while Earl cussed and fired rapidly, Clint loosened his cinch and said to the exhausted gelding, "They'll have to kill me before I run you another mile like that, old friend. This is where we make our stand. You've done your part, now, I reckon it's time that I did mine."

Clint yanked his rifle out of its scabbard. He levered a shell into the chamber and hurried back to join Earl. They were going to make a stand that these Apache would never forget. And even if they lost, the price would be very, very costly.

Clint dropped down onto one knee and sighted in on the first Indian. He took a deep breath and squeezed the trigger and the man lifted off his pony as if pulled by an invisible wire.

"Nice shooting," Earl grunted. "And if we just had us a cannon or a Gatling gun, maybe we'd get outta this alive!"

There was some truth to the ranch foreman's words. Before Clint could get off another shot, the Apache were flinging themselves off their ponies and disappearing into the heavy brush. They would stalk forward and offer very little target. Most likely, they'd wait until dusk the next day to attack, when the shadows were long and the light tricky and deceptive.

Then, they'd come in as silent as ghosts until the very final moment.

TWENTY-EIGHT

"I can smell them they are so damned close now," Earl whispered, his head moving back and forth, birdlike. "They'll be right on top of us before we even know they are there. I still say we ought to get the hell outta here fast!"

But the Gunsmith shook his head. "We stay and fight. Out there in the dark, we'd either get separated or else run our horses into a cactus plant or maybe a deep arroyo. This is where we stay, Earl. The three of us."

"I ain't running nowhere, not without 'Miss Covington, I ain't!" Chet said grimly. The kid had awakened soon after they'd reached the safety of these boulders. Now he seemed to be back to normal and Clint was mighty glad to have him by his side. Chet had not asked who'd picked his unconscious body off the desert floor. He'd known without asking.

"Let me tell you something about her," Earl said harshly. "I been thinking about this for days now, and the truth of it is, Chet, Lucy Covington ain't going to ever favor someone who works for her pa. She sees us as common working cowboys and that kind of man ain't never going to be good enough in her eyes."

"That's crazy talk!" Chet said, instantly defending the girl he idolized.

"No it ain't. Look at our gunfighter friend here. We work like dogs for Mr. Covington for years and along comes this fancy fella showing off his stuff. Before you can blink twice, Lucy goes right out and spreads her legs for him the very first night!"

Clint started to reach for the man's throat but Chet beat him to it. The kid was so incensed that, for an instant, his maniacal strength matched that of the much more powerful foreman. But Earl broke loose and swung a crunching blow that almost took Chet's head off. Before Earl could finish his work, Clint jammed his gun in the foreman's throat.

"Touch him again, I'll pull the trigger," Clint said in a way that left no doubt he'd do it. "Make another reference to Lucy that I don't like, I'll kill you for that too."

Earl's lip curled with contempt. "You need me as much as I need you. All three of us got to stick together to have any damn chance at all of getting out of Mexico alive."

"That may be the truth," Clint said agreeably, "but if I were you, I wouldn't stake my life on it."

Chet shook his head and tried to work his jaw. He spat out a tooth and blood. Then, he rolled away and stared out into the darkness saying, "Earl, I used to admire you. But not anymore. You ain't worth spit in a fix. A man couldn't trust you for a minute. We get out of this, I mean to take my gun to you."

Earl laughed. "Kid, you'll have to get in line behind the Gunsmith. And right now, he's in line behind a whole mess of Apache out there."

"Either way," Chet said evenly, "you're. . . ."

Whatever he was about to finish saying was interrupted as a blood-thirsty cry filled the night air and the Apache came at them out of the darkness.

Clint, Earl and Chet opened fire and took a return fire. Bullets and arrows came in at them from all directions to strike rock and ricochet away into the night. An Apache landed between them. He lunged for Earl and Clint shot him before he could plunge his knife into the foreman's back. A bullet whined meanly off a rock spraying Chet in the face with needle-sharp splinters. The kid was momentarily blinded and had the presence to duck or he would have been killed in the next few minutes.

Suddenly, like a giant lid slamming down on the desert, there was nothing but silence. Clint waited hearing his heartbeat loudly in his ears. He reloaded and the other two men took his example and did the same. Minutes passed by without a sound and then Earl whispered, "We beat them back. Maybe they're going to give up on us!"

"Not likely," Clint said in a hushed voice. "They're going to let the heat and the sun grind us down and then try again."

"How soon?"

"They don't care," Clint said. "However long it takes before we can't see or swallow or think. Then they'll walk in and take us easily."

"Jesus Christ!" Earl said hotly. "Then what's the point in waiting here until our horses are dead and we are dying of thirst. We ain't got enough water in our canteens to last us and our horses two days."

"I wouldn't give it that long," Clint said, rolling around to put his back to the warm rock and then shake his canteen. It was, at best, only half-full. Duke would drink that in one thirsty slurp and not have near enough to last through tomorrow.

They were in a real tight fix. Clint remembered old Ed Brisco talking about just such a fix he'd been in once. Only then it had been the Texas Panhandle and Comanche. Same situation, though. Trapped without water. Scorching heat of midsummer. No hope of help arriving.

"You know what Ed Brisco would do in a spot like this?" Clint asked.

"What?" Chet replied.

"He'd do what was least expected. Ed would have attacked these Indians. Cut right through them and tried to scatter their ponies."

Chet leaned closer. In the moonlight, his face was very pale, almost luminous. There were thin streaks of blood from the places where the bullet-splintered rock had cut him. "And then what?"

"Then we go back to the camp and see if Lucy is there. If she is, we take her back to her ranch."

"You think we could?" For the first time in days, there was excitement in Chet's voice.

"I don't know. All I'm sure of is that if we stay here we'll get weaker and they'll get stronger. And I'm not of a mind to let Duke die of thirst."

"Then let's do it," Earl said, starting to turn and crawl back to the horses.

"Not yet," Clint said. "Let's wait until just before daylight. "That way, if we do get through it will be in the darkness and by the time we reach their camp, it will be light enough to spot Lucy in a big hurry."

"Hot damn!" Chet said, rubbing his hands together with enthusiasm. "I just know this is going to work."

Even Clint was affected by the younger man's optimism. "I think it might at that," he said. "The only problem is, we have to figure out where their horses are out there in the darkness. Won't do any good to break through just to have the Apache right back on our tails."

"You leave the horses to me," Chet said. "I'm going out there and find them."

"Uh-uh," Clint said. "On foot, in the dark, you wouldn't stand a chance."

Chet wiped his face and looked at Clint in the moonlight. "I know you're the boss. And I most certainly do owe you my life. But our only chance is on me finding the horses and getting in among them. I can scatter them after I get on one and. . . ."

"You're talkin' nonsense," Earl hissed. "Those are Injun ponies out there. They're used to Indian smell. Not a white man's! They won't let you within fifty feet of 'em."

Chet had already thought about that. He moved over to the dead Apache and silently removed the man's shirt and a scarf that was tied around his neck. The Apache had an old army hat which Chet reluctantly exchanged with his own Stetson. He even pulled off the Indian's almost knee-high fringed moccasins and pulled them on after removing his boots.

"I hate to give up the hat," he said sorrowfully. "It was a good one, almost new. But the boots, well, they had big holes in the bottoms and were shot to hell anyway."

Clint smiled. "Boy, if you think you can do it, go on ahead with my blessings. And if you do succeed, I got a feeling that Angus Covington will buy you another hat and boots—as fine as can be found. And if he doesn't, I will.''

Chet grinned from ear to ear. "I'll get those horses," he promised. "You've never seen anyone that can move among horses like me, no matter how wild or crazy they are. Horses are horses. They know which men can be trusted. Which not. I'll do it and when you hear my gun, that's the signal to come bustin' on outta here."

Clint nodded. It was a terrible chance that the kid was taking, but it was probably their only one. Clint looked at them and said, "Let's rest. Each of us take an hour watch. I'll take the first and the last."

Neither one of them were of a mind to argue and they were both snoring within minutes. They are sure trusting souls, Clint thought with wry amusement.

I don't figure I'll sleep a wink this night. Not when there's a better than even chance it will be my last.

TWENTY-NINE

Clint kept watch until he guessed it was about four o'clock in the morning. Then, he woke Chet and took him to one side so that they could talk in private.

"What you are doing has to be done," Clint said. "And I'd do it myself only I know that you stand a better chance."

Chet grinned. "What's the matter? Feeling guilty, are you? You've saved my life once. If I can save your hide and Lucy's, then it'll be worth any price."

Clint knew the 'any price' meant the kid's life.

"If we get out of this, I'm going to tell Lucy what a fool she is not to have noticed you."

Chet rubbed the toe of his mocassin around in the dirt. "I'm afraid that Earl is right. I'm just not on her level. Never will be. Lucy and I . . . well, we've always been like brother and sister. Hell, I'm even a couple years younger than she is."

"You're a damn good man," Clint said. "A few years one way or the other don't make any difference."

"Not to you or me, maybe, but it does to Lucy. I don't mind so much. Being brother and sister is the next best thing to man and wife, ain't it?"

Clint just nodded though it seemed to him that 'the

next best thing' as Chet had put it, was a hell of a poor
second choice.

"Just watch yourself out there."

"I will." Chet stuck out his hand. "Win or lose, I got
to say that I sure read you wrong when we met the first
time. I know it was my jealousy that got in the way of
my good sense. But I can see what Lucy saw in you.
Why she chose you right away. You're the first real gunfighter I ever knew. To tell you the truth, I thought all
of 'em were backshooters. Men without much character
or guts but with a fast gunhand. I was wrong. You
risked your life for me. Makes me proud to have the
chance to do the same for you tonight."

They shook and Clint didn't trust his voice even to
wish the kid good luck before he left to vanish into the
sagebrush and rocks.

"That dumb sonofabitch don't have a chance," Earl
said contemptuously. "I give him less than five minutes
before they've got him skewered and roasting over a
pit."

Clint reached down and grabbed Earl by the throat.
"Shut up!" he hissed. "Before I waste a badly needed
bullet and put you out of your misery!"

Earl shut up. Clint turned his back on the man knowing that, under different circumstances, such action
would be fatal. But not early this morning with a pack
of Indians on the prowl. He leaned his cheek against a
rock and stared out into the night. A thin cloud had
covered the moon. It looked like dirty gauze wrapped
around the mantle of a lamp. But maybe the cloud was a
good sign. It would help Chet move through the Apache
to the horses. Give him that one chance in a hundred.
Maybe.

●   ●   ●

Chet moved out of the rocks dressed and smelling like
an Apache. He had listened to the night sounds, caught
the nicker of horses off to the right near a huge cactus
that loomed above the desert floor. Chet did not know
how the Apache kept their horses in a situation like this.
They might be hobbled, or tethered or even contained in
a makeshift rope corral. The latter would be his pref-
erence for that would make scattering them easiest and
quickest.

He had left his rifle but his sixgun was clenched
tightly in his fist. Chet was sweating heavily as he
hugged the ground and slithered silently down from the
rocks and into the brush. He did not expect to live. That
did not bother him so much because the Gunsmith
didn't give them much of a chance to live either. Chet
knew that, in this kind of a situation, there was no sense
in kidding yourself about surviving.

He glanced up at the moon. The cloud that covered it
was dragging slowly across its face. Chet figured he had
another fifteen or twenty minutes and then the desert
floor would become very bright. That did not give him a
hell of a lot of time to cover the necessary distance.

He placed his hand on something that moved. Before
he could lift it, the movement stung him. He reacted by
clenching his hand over the thing and that was when he
realized he'd been stung by a scorpion. Not usually
fatal, they still could make a man dizzy and sick. Chet
bit back the urge to swear at his carelessness and bad
luck. The pain was so strong it almost made him gag.
He laid his head down on his forearm, wanting to crush
the scorpion and yet thinking that it would be damned
useful to move any Apache that might block his path.

And one did. He sensed the man up in front of him
and Chet was only too happy to lob the wriggling and
highly agitated scorpion over the brush in the Apache's

direction. The Indian grunted, thrashed and crabbed off, slapping at his body. Chet grinned through his own pain and continued his crawl forward. Whenever he felt a flash of heat or sickness, he stopped, laid his head down for a moment and waited for it to pass.

The moon slipped out from behind the clouds and found him at the edge of a small clearing that occupied the base of that towering cactus plant. Chet saw the horses. They were guarded by only one Apache and the man was close. The horses were hobbled with a piece of rawhide stretched between their front pasterns. One of the ponies sensed his presence and snorted spookily.

The Apache sprang to grab its nostrils and that's when Chet rose to his feet, took three racing steps and clubbed him with his sixgun. The guard fell. The horses danced nervously.

"Easy," Chet crooned ever so softly. "Easy, boys." He slipped among them. There were about a dozen, all different colors, all wretchedly thin. Chet's hand brushed their coats, glided smoothly across their soft muzzles. Quieted them instantly. The entire process took less than a minute and then he was using his knife to slice the rawhide strips that served as hobbles.

Chet stayed right in the center of the Indian ponies. A convulsion shook him and sweat burst out across his face. The poison. He felt himself starting to get dizzy and he grabbed the mane of one of the ponies and hung on.

The animal spooked. It tried to pull away. The suddenness of the movement caught Chet off balance and he staggered. Then the convulsion passed as quickly as it hit him, and Chet steadied himself. His practiced eye gauged every pony in the band and chose the strongest. He went to it and then began to tie together the rawhide strips he had cut. When he had a piece about five feet long, he made a loop which he slipped over the animal's muzzle. Then he used the remainder of the strip as reins.

An Apache who had heard the disturbance caused by Chet's earlier convulsion stepped into the cleared space. He saw Chet, knew instantly that none of his own people stood so tall. He started to raise his rifle and Chet shot him. The Apache was knocked back into the brush. Chet swung onto the thin back of his pony and shouted, "Ya-hoo!"

He drummed his heels against the pony's ribs and sent it slamming into the others. They scattered in the right direction and he followed them yelling like a crazy man and watching those poor, starved ponies race through the brush.

"Run!" he yelled. "Run as far as you can and don't let yourselves ever be caught again!"

The freed ponies seemed to understand. Released from their cruel service, they ran with all their strength. It was a glorious sight, Chet thought, as he rode bareback chasing those ponies down a long valley. And he would have followed them for miles except another powerful spasm shook his body and made it stiffen. For an instant, he lost control of his arms and legs. And to his great humiliation, the greatest bronc-buster in the Arizona Territory tumbled off the galloping horse just like a greenhorn.

Chet hit the ground and rolled. He lay still hearing the sound of the receding hooves. Far behind he could also hear guns booming in the night.

He vomited into the dirt and wondered if he had saved the life of the famous Gunsmith. Now wouldn't that have been something to tell the boys around a campfire.

THIRTY

When the shot rang out, Clint and Earl were ready to ride. Clint had the pack horse's lead rope wrapped around his saddlehorn and his Stetson was pulled down low on his forehead.

About three in the morning he'd given Duke and the other horses all but the last few sips of their canteens. When Earl woke up and discovered what he'd done, the man had been furious but Clint had just stated a cold, hard fact—a white man afoot in this country was a dead man.

Now, as the firing started, Clint let Duke charge out of their rocky fortress. The big black guided them forward at a racing speed. Gunflashes winked like cat's eyes in the night. Clint's gun flashed back. An Apache seemed to spring from the earth and he leapt for Duke's reins. The gelding bowled him over with its powerful shoulder. It was over in less then thirty seconds and then suddenly, they were out in the open and racing like the wind. Free and alive.

Behind him, Clint heard Earl yelp with joy. But it was Chet the Gunsmith was searching for. He followed a thin trail of dust toward the original Apache camp and let Duke run almost two miles before the animal snorted

and veered suddenly. Clint had to grab his saddlehorn
or he might have lost his seat.

He hauled on the reins knowing that Duke would not
have shied like that without a very good reason. It only
took a minute to find Chet pushing himself to his knees
and lifting his head about the line of sagebrush. He
swayed drunkenly, then climbed up to his feet.

"Are you hurt bad?" Clint yelled, jumping out of the
saddle and running to the kid's side. "Where were you
hit!"

Chet shook his head with embarrassment. He held up
the palm of his left hand and it was swollen up to twice
its normal size. "Scorpion got me," he choked bitterly.
"Ain't that one for the books? A whole passle of
Apache after my scalp, and damned if I don't get nailed
by a damned scorpion!"

Clint let out a sigh of relief. "You'll feel a whole lot
better come tomorrow. Right now, why don't we get
you back on Duke and keep traveling. We ought to be
able to find you another horse out here somewhere."

"I dunno," Chet said. "Them ponies I stampeded
outta here looked like they was scalded. Might run all
the way to Central America or someplace nearly as
far."

Clint got the kid into the saddle and they rode after
Earl who hadn't even bothered to wait.

Chet said with disgust, "You might as well kill him
now as later, Gunsmith. He's just waiting for the moment to kill you."

"I know that," Clint said over his shoulder. "But
there's Lucy to take care of first. Once we get her out of
Mexico, then Earl and I can settle our personal dif-
ferences."

"Apache camp can't be more than four or five miles

up ahead. What are we fixin' to do when we get there?''

"Just hope that we can find Lucy—along with a couple of extra horses. Then ride north as fast as we can."

"We'll need more than our share of luck to find water."

Clint nodded. They sure would. But they could take their fill at the Apache meadow camp. Let the horses drink deep and then make their dash north. "Chet, whatever comes our way, it can't be much worse than the mess you just helped us get out of back in those rocks."

"Don't say that, Gunsmith. In my own short but exciting life, everytime I thought things couldn't possibly get worse, I was proved dead wrong."

"Well I sure hope this time you're wrong." Clint reloaded his gun and set Duke into a steady trot. He wished the animal didn't have to carry double, but they just couldn't afford to throw away their stockpile of extra guns, ammunition and dynamite. Not until they had Lucy, and then it wouldn't matter. The pack horse would become her saddle mount and they'd make a run for it.

First light of dawn and the Apache camp was deserted. All three men swore as they refilled their canteens and let the horses drink. The Apache had left in a huge hurry. Their campfire was still burning and pieces of meat sizzled and smoked.

"They went southwest," Clint said. "They can't be more than an hour ahead of us. They'll be traveling slow and on foot. Women and children. We ought to be able to catch them within two hours even with Duke carrying double. But we'll need to spell him every few miles."

"We don't even know if Lucy is with them," Earl said. In a dejected and cutting tone he added, "I'm beginning to think she ain't."

"Doesn't matter what you think, dammit!" Chet shouted. His face was flushed and Clint knew that the scorpion's poison was making him feverish.

Clint stepped between them. "Get on your horse," he ordered the big foreman. "In case you've forgotten, there are a whole passle of Apache behind us and you can bet your life they are coming fast."

"Without horses they. . . ."

"They can still run us down if we aren't careful to keep moving," Clint said brusquely. "Let's ride."

Earl's jaw muscles rippled but he wisely said nothing. The Gunsmith was fresh out of patience. He climbed up behind Chet and they headed out of the meadow knowing it would be a long, hard ride. They sure weren't cheered by the knowledge that they were heading deeper and deeper into Mexico.

THIRTY-ONE

They overtook the fleeing Apache in less than two hours. It was nothing Clint would be proud to recount. They simply topped a low rise of land and there they were, a poor, ragged band of women, old men and children hurrying across the land.

"Look!" Earl shouted, "ain't that Lucy!"

It was. She was being half-led, half-dragged by mounted squaws who had tied ropes around her neck. Now, as the Apache people looked back and saw them coming, the squaws beat their scarecrow horses into a shambling trot. Children shrieked in fear and younger women grabbed their babies and began to scatter into the heavy brush.

Clint saw Earl tear his rifle out of his scabbard and lever in a shell. "No!" Clint shouted. "I don't want any of them hurt!"

"Oh yeah, well look what they're doin' to Lucy! They're trying to drag her to death!"

There was some truth in that. The squaws were forcing their ponies to trot faster and faster. They were trying to beat the starving animals into a gallop. Clint could see Lucy trying vainly to run fast enough to keep herself from falling. He could hear the squaws screeching as they beat at their Indian ponies.

"Shoot their horses!" he yelled, yanking his own rifle from under Chet's leg and throwing it to his shoulder.

Both he and Earl fired at almost the same moment but, unfortunately, they both shot the same pony. It went down and now Lucy was strung up as though along a clothesline. The ropes snapped taut around her neck and then Clint fired a desperate shot that dropped the remaining horse but not before Lucy was whipped between both dying animals. Clint saw her reach up and grab her throat as if to tear the ropes away. One of the squaws hit the ground and came up with a knife. Clint sent a bullet in her direction and the old woman skidded to a stop, reversed herself and took off running.

Chet was off Duke and running before the horse even stopped. He reached Lucy first. She was choking to death, trying to loosen the ropes round her throat. Chet had his knife out and somehow, he got its blade between the rope and her throat.

Clint was paying so much attention to Lucy that he almost didn't see the first squaw whose pony they'd shot come charging forward with her knife. The woman screeched, intent on stabbing both Chet and Lucy. Earl jumped off his horse. He swung his rifle to kill her but Clint spurred Duke forward and managed to knock the old squaw down and shield her from Earl's rifle.

"Outta my way!" Earl bellowed. "Or so help me, I'll shoot you right now!"

The squaw sensed the fight between the two men. She tried to crawl past Clint and his horse but the Gunsmith blocked her path.

"Move, damn you!"

Clint swung around to tell Earl that it wasn't necessary to kill the old woman. They could save Lucy and

Chet from her knife without bloodshed. But something in Earl's face told him that the ranch foreman had reached the limit of his reason. He'd been waiting for this moment too long and now that Lucy was found, he figured he did not need the Gunsmith anymore.

Earl swung the rifle from the squaw toward Clint who drew his sixgun and fired. Their shots joined and the rifle bullet sent Clint's hat spinning. The ranch foreman took Clint's bullet in the gunhand and his weapon was ripped away, taking his trigger finger with it.

Earl bellowed in pain and grabbed his wrist.

The squaw froze. She looked at Clint and then at the wounded man who had been about to kill her. Some strange word meant for Clint alone was torn from her lips and then she whirled and went scurrying after her people.

Clint dismounted and walked over to Earl. He had not wanted to shoot the fool because they would need all the firepower they could muster to escape Mexico. Clint had sworn to hold off their showdown until Lucy was safe but now that was a promise shot to hell. Earl was bleeding heavily and the bullet had passed through the end of his thumb and then the palm of his hand. He'd survive and even use the hand, but never again without pain and some stiffness. "You fool," Clint said, as he pressed his handkerchief over the wound. "Why did you do it?"

Earl grimaced. "Because I couldn't wait. I still can't."

Clint took Earl's rifle away. "I can't trust you any longer."

Lucy looked like hell. There was a big rope burn around her throat and her face was thin and haggard.

Her once beautiful complexion was now burnt by sun
and her shiny hair was dull, tangled with dirt and
branches. Along one side of her face was a jagged lacer-
ation that had become infected and would leave a thin
but visible scar. It was clear that Lucy had fought and
paid dearly for her refusal to be obedient to her captors.
Her arms were covered with bruises. It was like looking
at a stranger, except for Lucy's eyes which were every
bit as fiercely independent as he had remembered.
Those eyes told Clint that, no matter what the Apache
had done to this woman, they had not yet broken her
spirit.

"You shouldn't have tried to kill her," Lucy said, her
eyes boring into Earl.

"But she was trying to kill you!" Earl choked in
disbelief. "I saved your life."

Lucy shook her head. "No. Chet and the Gunsmith
did. Take a look over there."

They all followed her gaze. They saw an old man with
a very big rifle, a rifle that Clint recognized immediately
as a buffalo gun. "He would have killed me if you had
shot the squaw. It would have been my life for hers.
That's their code. You kill an Apache woman, they kill
one of yours. Earl, you almost cost me my life."

The foreman blinked. Tried to grab his rifle from
Clint and kill someone. Clint didn't think it would have
mattered to Earl who he shot—the old Apache who
watched from a distance, Chet, Lucy, himself. Earl just
wanted blood. So when the man cried out in madness
and frustration, Clint brought the rifle's walnut stock
up in a sweeping motion that caught Earl solidly under
the jaw. The foreman dropped like a stunned ox.

"We don't have much time," Chet said. "We have to
get out of here."

But Lucy hesitated. "There's something I have to tell you first," she said. "Before you came the other night, there was another captive. A Mexican woman. She had been treated even worse than I was. Her courage set the example I tried to follow. Once, when the squaws were beating me, she picked up a handful of rocks and threw them in order to divert the squaws from me to herself. Later, she told me about you, Clint."

He took a deep breath. "Her name was Juanita, wasn't it?"

Lucy nodded. "She had a little brother she was trying to protect. Some of the Apache took her and the small boy away two days before you tried to rescue me but were stopped in the wash."

"Where did they take them?"

"To find Geronimo," Lucy said. "I think they went farther north."

"Juanita told me not to tell you about her and the boy. She said what happened was God's will. I think. . . ." Lucy drew in a ragged breath. "Juanita was in love with you, Clint."

Clint's head swung around. "Did she say that?"

"No, but I could tell."

Clint's fists knotted and he suddenly felt a hundred years old. "I just can't leave her and that boy to them," he whispered. "Chet, you can take Duke and the best horse you have. Get Lucy out of this land and don't look back until. . . ."

"Clint!" Her voice cracked like a bullwhip.

He stared at her.

"We're not going back without you—or Juanita and the young boy. I couldn't live with myself either."

"Are you crazy?" Earl rasped. "Has everyone but me gone mad?"

Clint did not take his eyes off the battered, sunburnt face of Lucy Covington whose jaw was set with determination. There would be no changing this woman's mind. "Okay," he said. "That's it, then. Chet?"

"Try and stop me from coming along with you," the young man said in a voice thick with emotion.

"Earl?"

The big man tore his eyes from his bullet-ruined hand. "What chance would I have trying to make it back to the border alone!"

"About as much chance as we'll have going after Geronimo," Clint replied.

Earl swore long and hard. He was beaten. And though he didn't want any part of it, he was going to have to join them on Geronimo's trail.

THIRTY-TWO

With Caddo and his band of Apache on their back trail and Geronimo heading even deeper into Mexico, things could not have been any bleaker. Clint wished like hell that they could have stayed at the desert oasis a few days to rest and gather their strength for whatever lay ahead. But there was no time. The Apache would soon recapture at least some of their ponies and even those on foot would continue the pursuit.

They bandaged Earl's shattered gunhand and risked letting their horses eat for two precious hours. Then, they rode out in the heat of the day, staring into a trackless land and wondering where they would find Geronimo.

Because it was impossible to pick up Juanita's trail, Clint had it in mind to head for Magdelena and find the girl's parents. They would be keeping track of Geronimo, and they might be able to help in some way.

Clint did not know the exact direction of that Mexican town, but he did know they had about a hundred miles of low mountain ranges and desert to cross before they would come to the Rio Magdelena. Once they found it, they could always ask directions. In this country, wherever there was water, there were villages and

farmers. Mexico was so dry in the northern provinces
that the peons were forced to overcrowd the irrigable
lands.

It was a hard trip and it took them two days to climb
and scratch their way to Rio Magdelena. By the time
they reached it, their canteens were empty and their
horses staggering with thirst. They decided to make
camp early and rest up for tomorrow when they would
seek out the Sanchez family.

While Earl and Chet set up camp, Lucy and Clint
walked along the bank of the river until they found a
grassy place to sit and talk.

"We could not have lasted another day," Lucy said,
voicing Clint's exact thoughts. "I don't know how you
timed it so well."

"Dumb luck," Clint replied. "Juanita had described
this country, and I have been here before but most of it
is country a man tries to forget, rather than remember."

"Do you still think that Caddo and his warriors are
on our trail?"

They moved out onto a sandbar in the fading light of
day. The water sounded like gentle music. Clint and
Lucy took off their boots and felt the cool water on
their feet.

"I wish we could stay here just like this," Lucy said,
turning to look at him, "with you and this nice old
river."

"You'd get tired of me and I'd get tired of the river,"
Clint said jokingly. He studied her face.

The purplish bruises were gone already and the
scratches were healing quickly. He wished that she had
not suffered that thin cut across her cheek and that it
had healed better. But he decided that the resulting scar
would fade with time. It would be barely noticeable,

and would not diminish her beauty.

She knelt before him. "I'm not very pretty anymore, am I, Clint?"

He had been expecting something like this and welcomed it. A woman who had been used as a slave and been forced to submit to an Indian warrior was bound to have suffered mentally. During his years as a lawman, Clint had seen the devastation that raped women suffered. In a case like Lucy's, the damage could be devastating to someone with less steel.

He took her sunburnt face and cupped it in his hands. "You'll be as pretty as ever when you've had a chance to recover."

"I'll be scarred for life."

"Lucy, your face will bear a slight scar, but it won't matter to someone who falls in love with you. We're all scarred, every single one of us. It doesn't matter; the only scars that count are the ones we suffer inside. Don't let any of this hurt you there."

"But how can a woman who has been . . . used by a man like Caddo not be scarred inside?"

"You fought him. There was nothing more that you could do."

"I know that. My face will always serve as a reminder. I wanted him to kill me. He wouldn't but only because I was valuable to him. Am I valuable to you, Clint?"

"Of course." Clint pitched a pebble into the slow moving river. "You know who you should think about as the kind of a man you need to marry?"

"You."

"No, Chet."

Her eyes widened. "He's . . . he's like a kid brother!"

"He's deeply in love with you, Lucy. And there's

nothing brotherly about his love.''

"But . . . but he's little more than a boy.''

"Wrong again. Maybe he had some boy in him when we left Arizona, but not anymore. He's a man. A man who'd give his life to making you happy.''

Lucy smiled. Shook her head as if the idea of Chet and her in a way unlike brother and sister was something she could never accept. Clint understood that, but sometimes you had to plant seeds to see things important grow. From now on, he would just bet that Lucy would be watching Chet a little closer. Seeing him in just a slightly different light. And what she'd see, if they lived to get out of Mexico, she would like.

"I have an idea," Lucy said taking his hand.

"I'm listening.''

"Let's go for a long swim. I want to wash all the Apache off me. That along with all the miles of dust and sweat.''

"A fine idea and one that I was going to suggest myself,'' he said.

She undressed slowly and he saw that her body was much thinner than the time they had made love near the Covington Ranch.

"What I wouldn't give for soap,'' she said wistfully, as she stood up and waded out into the water.

Clint shucked his boots and clothes. He laid his six-gun on top of everything and went in after her. It was almost dark now and the temperature was still in the eighties, but the water had definitely cooled down. He wasted no time but instead, dove in with a splash. Lucy swam to his side.

For a few minutes, they played in the water, taking turns dunking each other. Then, they began to wash each other. Then the laughing stopped and things got

serious. They floated onto a sandbar which was sub-
merged by a few inches of river water.

Lucy pulled him close and they lay side by side for a
few moments, lazily stroking each other with the sand
and the water, feeling their bodies respond to the touch
and the delightful sense of water flowing over their skin.
Then Lucy was kissing him feverishly, pulling him onto
her.

"Make love to me!" she whispered urgently. "I need
you so bad!"

He knew what she meant. Knew that she hoped he
could drive away some of the humiliation and degradation that she had suffered under Caddo's hard, insistent
body.

Clint wasted no time. He had taken a lot of women,
but never one quite in this position. It was exciting and
he slipped wetly into her.

"Oh," she breathed, "yes!"

She was like a starving animal and he fed her well.
He gave her the full length of himself and because she
seemed to want him to do it to her tenderly, the Gunsmith forced his loins to move in a slow ellipsis that tan-
talized and slowly built her to a trembling frenzy.

Lucy stiffened and held him for a long moment and
he marveled at her control until, suddenly, her body
began to buck and pump in the shallow water. Her legs
were kicking and splashing. She bit his shoulder and
then cried, "Hard now, Clint. Do it to me hard!"

And he did. It was so easy. His own body was aching
for release too. He began to thrust powerfully and soon,
the river and sand was churning with their desire. When
they came, water was splashed everywhere.

Lucy cried out in pleasure and locked her thighs
around his driving hips. Clint ducked his head in the

river and roared with satisfaction and filled her with his seed.

Afterward, when they were dressed, she was smiling. "I feel clean again, Clint. As clean as the driven snow. And it wasn't just the river. It was you as well."

That made the Gunsmith feel good. For the first time in a good long while he completely forgot about Geronimo and what lay ahead.

THIRTY-THREE

At a village named Rosario, they learned that Magdelena was about twenty miles downriver.

"How come we never go north," Earl said bitterly. "How come it's always south for us?"

Clint glanced at the man. The bullet-shattered hand had been an agony but his pain and hatred now made him seem more formidable, rather than less. Pure, stupid brawn, Clint had never worried too much about. You could always shoot or pistol whip a two-fisted brawling giant like Earl Sturges. But when men got hurt and festered inside, sometimes they became diabolical as hell. Devious and crafty. That was the kind of a man you worried the most about. Sooner or later, Earl was going to find an unguarded moment and try to strike a killing blow.

Chet understood that his own life was also in danger from the wounded foreman. Maybe, Clint thought, between the two of them, they could manage to keep from getting a bullet in the back.

They rode up the river, passing several villages and farms. The Mexican people watched them with suspicion. Strangers to their land were almost always the bearers of misfortune.

When they reached Magdelena, they found it to be a town of about two thousand, easily strong enough in numbers to defend itself against Apache attacks. There was a plaza in the center of the town, complete with wooden benches. Huge trees shaded old men who sat smoking and arguing among themselves. In the middle of the plaza was a fountain, probably fed by the first communal well.

Magdelena looked prosperous compared to most of the villages in this part of Mexico. There were shops and even a vendor who sold them tortillas with some kind of hot sauce that Clint found interesting but which made his eyes water. Clint asked several people as to the whereabouts of Senor Sanchez, but they all hurried away crossing themselves.

"What is the matter with them?" Lucy asked.

"I don't know." Clint frowned. "My guess is that it is because of the Sanchez family's misfortunes. There's the chapel up at the end of the street. Let's try and find a priest who speaks a little English."

They dismounted at the chapel and tied their horses at the hitch rail. It was a small, dimly lit church with an altar and the stations of the cross painted on all the adobe walls. Behind the church was a walled-in courtyard filled with lovely flowers and a magnificent melon and tomato patch. It was in the courtyard that they found Father Garcia chewing his way through an entire roast chicken. A corpulent man in his fifties, round with double chins and a belly that hung over the tasseled rope around his tent-sized black robes. When he saw the Americans approach, his eyes widened and he tried to hide the chicken and wipe his face free of grease all in one swift motion. He was successful in neither attempt but did not seem flustered in the least. He swallowed noisily, smacked his lips and grinned widely.

"Ahh!" he proclaimed, rising with some difficulty and plodding toward them with his fat hands outstretched. "Americanos! Welcome to Magdelena. What a pleasure!"

He really seemed to mean it and Clint was glad to have found someone who could speak fluent English. "Thank you," he said, making the introductions all around.

When the priest saw Lucy's face, he blinked with concern. "You need medicine for that. I will get some for you right away!"

He clapped his hands and a small Mexican boy came running. He bowed to the priest who instructed him in Spanish so rapid that Clint only caught the sketchiest part of the conversation. The boy shot out of the courtyard on his errand of mercy. "He will be back soon, Senorita."

"What about my hand?" Earl snarled.

"It is the will of God. You will perhaps shoot no more, eh, Senor?"

Clint and Chet both stifled grins. This priest was a good judge of bad men.

He gave them something cool to drink from his cellar, a mixture of wine and something even more potent. The afternoon sun filtered softly through the shade trees and Clint would have liked to have remained, but the thought of Juanita Sanchez and her little brother prompted him to interrupt a long monologue by the priest about the extreme piety of his congregation.

"Father, excuse me, but we are in a hurry."

The priest did not seem in the least bit offended by the interruption. "Senor! No one hurries in Mexico! That is the great fault of your countrymen. They hurry too much. Always, they rush this way and that.''

To demonstrate, the priest swept his flabby arms around in rapid circles.

"You are right, of course," Clint said. "But we are here seeking to help Senorita Juanita Sanchez and her small brother, who have both fallen into the hands of the Apache."

The priest's smile died. He crossed himself and bent his head in a moment of prayerful silence. When he looked up, his eyes were wet with tears. "We have already said a mass for them. I have given them the last rites."

"Are you sure they're dead?" Lucy cried. "I just saw them but a few days ago."

"They are dead. I have been told that they are to become members of Geronimo's band. If he does not kill them, sooner or later the Mexican army will. Those people are doomed. It is just a matter of time before they are all slaughtered like cattle. Their souls will not go to heaven without great burdens to unveil."

Lucy's anger flared. "Father! Juanita and her little brother have no sins to be forgiven. It was not their fault that they were captured by the Apache!"

"Can you be so sure of that? Are we not punished justly by our Creator? Maybe the punishment is to absolve the sins of our ancestors. I don't know. All I am sure of is that we pray for Juanita and poor, innocent little Alfredo. But in our minds, they are the same as dead."

"I don't accept that," Clint said roughly. "We've got a pack horse laden with trading goods and saddlebags stuffed with money. We figure to buy those two their freedom. All we want from you is any information you might have as to where we can find Geronimo."

Father Garcia smiled tolerantly. "Very well, perhaps you each have some sins to atone for yourselves. In that case, I will tell you that Geronimo is headed north again."

"North!" Clint looked at his companions. This was the first good piece of news that they had yet received.

"Si. We know that he and his band are moving toward their stronghold. We thank God they are leaving Mexico once again."

"They are going back to the United States?"

"God willing, yes. To the Mogollon Mountains in your New Mexico Territory."

Earl shook his head. "We passed within fifty miles of 'em on our way down here."

Lucy snapped. "Well excuse me for getting kidnapped! Maybe you're thinking you should have waited until Geronimo finally decided to ride north again!"

"That ain't what I was thinking!"

Lucy turned away from the big man. Earl was surely getting the message that he had totally fallen out of the woman's favor. He sure could not have held out much hope of marrying into the Covington Ranch money now.

"Please," the priest said. "You must stay and rest for a few days. Geronimo will wait. Men have been chasing him for years."

"We should go see Juanita's father and mother to tell them our plans."

"No," the priest said gently. "They have gone away and given their land to others. Their sorrow was so great, they could not bear to remain here any longer. They now live in Mexico City. It is better that way."

Clint shook his head. "They gave everything away?"

"Si. They were very sad. Perhaps, if you find their

children, they come and find them again. It would be
like being reborn again. A miracle from God."

"You make it sound as if we have no chance at all,"
Chet said.

The priest smiled sadly and crossed himself once
more. When he spoke, his words were very soft and
filled with sorrow. "If you go on Geronimo's trail, you
will have no chance. And you will die screaming for
God's mercy. I grant that it will come to you quickly
and that you will suffer no more."

They stayed that night in Magdelena, and for the first
time in weeks, Duke had fresh hay and grain.

He ate well and the Mexican children brushed his
coat, mane and tail until all the tangles were free. He
looked like a new horse, though it pained the Gunsmith
to see the way his ribs outlined his deep chest.

Clint rented a Mexican mule and while the others
were getting a much needed sleep, he rode the beast out
to the Sanchez ranch to see it for himself. What he saw
was a very, very poor little farm with a house made of
both adobe and thatched sticks. Father Garcia had been
too kind to say that the Sanchez ranch was worth prac-
tically nothing. It was on high ground far from the river
and water had to be hauled for the small patch of
vegetables. Most of the property was on a rocky moun-
taintop. In the moonlight, Clint had no trouble finding
the boundaries of that ranch and it could not have supported more than a half dozen cattle or horses.

He wondered how a family like that had survived,
managed to buy those nice saddles once owned by her
older brothers, Gregorio and Manuel. One thing for certain, they had not earned them farming on this land.

Clint reined the mule in and studied the silhouette of

the house for a long minute. Juanita had not exactly said her father was wealthy, but that was the impression she had given. Clint smiled. If he found her and little Alfredo and then managed to get them safely away from Geronimo perhaps he could persuade Lucy to give them a home and jobs on the Covington Ranch. And if not, he knew a few friends who might be able to help that brave young woman and her small brother. Juanita had saved his life, he was not going to let her and Alfredo Sanchez come back to find what little they'd once owned had been given away by their grieving parents.

THIRTY-FOUR

They rode north toward the border just as fast as their horses would carry them. After the long uncertainty about how far they would have to go into Mexico, the good fortune they now had—heading for New Mexico —seemed too good to be true. Even Earl's surly disposition had improved and he seemed to have made some kind of peace with himself and bided his time in silence. He took the Gunsmith's orders, did his share of the work each night in camp, and did not complain.

Sometimes, though, Clint caught the man staring at him and his eyes were a cold reminder that nothing had changed between them. That, and the fact that Earl was spending a lot of time on the trail practicing the draw and firing motion with his left hand.

They did not even realize they had crossed the border into the United States until four hard days later when they came upon the town of Lordsburg, New Mexico.

"Jesus, would you look at that!" Earl said, almost hoarse with his excitement. "I never thought we'd get out of that damned Mexico alive. But our luck held. What I want now is a bottle of whiskey and a . . ." he remembered that Lucy was among them and left the sentence unsaid though everyone knew what he wanted besides the drink.

They rode into Lordsburg and took rooms at the Monte Hotel. That day Chet, Lucy and Clint enjoyed the almost forgotten luxury of hot baths and real bars of soap. They sent out their clothes to be cleaned by a local Chinese laundryman who only charged them two bits and promised to have everything pressed and ready in the morning. Lucy bought some new clothes at the general store. Clint took charge of the ransom money which they now intended to use to buy Juanita and Alfredo. Lucy supported that plan completely, though she did comment that her father would not necessarily need to know that his five thousand dollars had not been used as intended.

"If he learned we spent all that money to buy the freedom of a Mexican woman and her little brother, he would roar so loud they could hear him in Salt Lake City," she said with a laugh. "Don't you agree with that, Chet?"

They were eating at the best cafe in town. Chet blushed despite the fact that their long hours together on the trail had caused a visible and healthy change in their relationship. The most obvious change was that the young man was not so much in awe of his boss's daughter. He even joked with Lucy now. It was a good sign and Clint did not fail to note that Lucy no longer treated him like a boy, or exactly like a little brother. Rather, she was starting to listen to him as if he were an equal and an interesting and highly knowledgeable young man who knew more about horses and mustanging than anyone she knew.

"I reckon I might go to Nevada, or maybe Wyoming,

and mustang," he said. "I sure would hate to leave your ranch, Lucy, but I need to see a change of country. I'm a little burned out on cactus and sagebrush."

"I can sure understand that," she said. "So am I. And Apache. If we survive Geronimo, I never want to see another one again."

"There are Shoshoni in Wyoming," Chet said. "But they're a whole lot friendlier. Not all Indians are like Geronimo and his raiders."

"I know that," Lucy replied. "And I love horses. Are there many up there where you're going?"

"Thousands," Chet said eagerly. "You see, the whole trick is to catch them. But I have a way . . . well, you seen me with horses so I don't have to explain anything. I been thinking about it for a long time and I got some ideas of my own to try. I just know that I can catch them. Start a ranch. Somewhere near the Wind River country. The grass grows waist high in summer. Lot of sweet smelling pines. Water tastes like sugar it's so clear and cold."

Lucy leaned forward. "Where did you learn all about that country?"

"Talking to men. But they weren't lying to me, I swear it. They say it's so green and pretty that it'd make an artist weep."

"That's beautiful the way you said that."

Chet studied his hands. "I write a little poetry, Lucy. I guess I've probably written about a hundred for you. Love poems."

Lucy swallowed. Clint looked from one to the other and decided it would be a good time to make his exit. He needed to buy a few supplies and talk to the sheriff. He had a feeling these two were just beginning to discover that they had a lot more in common than they'd imagined.

Sheriff Thompson studied him. "I sure wish you'd change your mind about going after that girl and her little brother. Gunsmith, I can't help you at all up there. Nobody will. Not for any price."

"That's all right. If we went up there with a bunch of men, they'd take it as a posse or scalp-hunters. But just the four of us with a pack horse for trading won't raise any problem to a chief like Geronimo."

"He might decide to kill you and take everything free."

"I don't think so. He needs traders to bring him guns, food, blankets, guns and ammunition. But I would like to leave the last two items I mentioned here in your office."

"You'd better. Army hears of you providing weapons and bullets to them Apache, they'd pitch you into a federal prison and never let you out!"

"Fine with me. Maybe we'll just take some blankets and the money."

"Ought to be enough. They're only two Mex."

Clint chose to ignore the slur. There were a lot of Mexican haters north of the border and the opposite was equally true the south of it. The United States and Mexico were two very different countries. They had been at war and would never forgive each other their losses. "You have any suggestions about where I ought to start looking?"

"Nope. They hide out up there in those mountains but they never stay put in one place so that the army can trap them. Geronimo will find you, Gunsmith. I hope he keeps you alive long enough to talk."

"I die hard," Clint said. "I just wish the girl would stay here."

"Make her."

"Lucy Covington?" Clint laughed outright. "You don't know the woman or you'd realize how ridiculous that suggestion is."

The lawman leaned forward across his desk. "Listen, man. You just tell her a hair-raising story about how Apache treat their slaves. What the squaws and the men do to them. The chiefs take the pretty ones and use them like whores!"

Clint felt the hair on the back of his neck rise. "I think she already knows that," he managed to say as he left the man's office.

THIRTY-FIVE

The Mogollon Mountains ran northwest for hundreds of miles and some of their peaks punched up from the New Mexico plateau to an elevation of over ten thousand feet. Armies could get lost in those mountains. They could follow them damn near all the way to Arizona Territory's Grand Canyon.

But now, on their third day out of Lordsburg, Clint had a feeling that Geronimo and his band of renegades were very close indeed. The trick was in getting close enough to make them understand that they wanted to buy Juanita and little Alfredo Sanchez for five thousand dollars.

Clint had allowed Earl the use of his gun but he'd kept the man's bullets. In an emergency, he could toss Earl cartridges and the man could reload in an instant. Maybe it wouldn't make sense to anyone else to carry an empty gun, but to Earl it was like a baby's pacifier.

"Hey!" Chet said. "I saw a movement up in those rocks."

"Apache?"

Chet nodded as five of them rode into view. "I think we found Geronimo and his boys. But I'm not sure that I'm too happy about it."

Clint rigged a white rag to his gunbarrel. He waved it back and forth.

Earl nudged his horse up beside Clint. "Give me some bullets, goddamn you!"

"Not yet," Clint said, never taking his eyes off the Indians. "The last thing we need is for you to open fire on these people. We wouldn't get a mile before they'd have us for supper."

Earl cussed, but he reined his animal away and waited. Clint glanced over at Lucy. She was pale, but her chin was up and she looked determined to go through with this. Considering what she had already endured with Caddo and his people, that showed Clint how much raw courage Lucy Covington possessed.

The Apache came forward. Clint studied the warrior in the lead. He knew instinctively that this was the most feared man in America. Geronimo. The great war chief was short but very powerfully built and rode a black horse. He wore little in the way of adornments or jewelry and his face was hard and impassive. He seemed to have no lips and the line of his mouth was pulled down at the corners. His hair was long, parted exactly down the center and then whacked off at shoulder length. His clothing was multi-colored. Something almost like a tunic was pulled down to his breeches. He wore the almost knee-length and traditional Apache moccasins. Geronimo carried a very good Winchester rifle and the sun glinted off a silver ring on his finger.

"Hold steady," Clint said. "I think he wants to palaver a few minutes before he decides whether to kill us or not."

Clint forced a smile. They all three did but the Apache seemed to wear a perpetual look of scorn. When they stopped, the Indians studied them for almost a full minute before Geronimo spoke. When he did, his English was rougher than that of Juanita Sanchez. "What you come for?"

Clint took a deep breath. He wished he could say something that would be well received. A compliment? No, that would infuriate this man. Forget the small talk. Get right to the point like he has. "I come to buy Mexican woman and her small brother. Their names are Juanita and Alfredo Sanchez. You have?"

The Apache chief studied him for a long time before he nodded his head. "Apache slave."

"No. My woman." Clint surprised himself. He had not expected to say that, but he sensed that any other claim or explanation would have been dismissed by this man. "My woman!"

Geronimo's black eyes flicked to Chet, Lucy and Earl. The question was evident. What did they want?

"Friends," Clint said.

"Stupid friends," Geronimo said, spitting both words out of his mouth like cherry pits. He studied Clint for another moment, then turned his horse and rode away. His men followed him.

"What are we supposed to do?" Chet hissed.

"I'm getting the hell outta here!" Earl said, wheeling his horse around and driving spurs into the animal.

"Let him go," Clint ordered. "He has no reason to stay. We're better off without him. Let's follow Geronimo. All right?"

They nodded and he was purely proud of them both. They might be riding to their deaths, but they were going to do it with courage and style.

"By the way," Clint said to Lucy. "I have forgotten to ask you something very important. And if we are about to die, I'd still like to know the answer."

"Then ask," Lucy said.

"It seems like a hundred years ago. But Chet told me

you had learned something new about Ed Brisco that
might help tell me who murdered him. Did you?"

"Yes. I know who murdered the sheriff of Broken
Lance."

"Well?"

"It was Roy Beyers. The man who tried to ambush
you in town. I got a long letter from his wife. I knew her
before Roy contracted gold fever. It seems that Sheriff
Brisco and Mrs. Beyers were close friends. Nothing
more. Roy Beyers used to beat his wife. Ed took pity on
the poor woman and tried to help her husband so that
he might give her a better life."

"He grubstaked Roy Beyers for a share of anything
he found. The man struck gold and then murdered Ed
rather than share their claim."

Lucy nodded. "I'm afraid that is exactly what happened. Mrs. Beyers was broken hearted but afraid to
even attend the sheriff's funeral. She knew her presence
might be misunderstood. That it would most surely
cause gossip and hurt Clair Morrison deeply. She fled to
Wichita where she has family."

Clint shook his head. So, the mystery was unraveled
and he had already killed his old friend Ed Brisco's
backshooting murderer. Good! At least if Geronimo
and his band killed him, justice would already have been
done.

"I always thought it was Earl Sturges," Clint mused
out loud. "I must be losing my lawman's instincts."

Lucy reached out and squeezed his hand. "Cheer
up," she managed to say as they followed the Apache,
"things can and very well may get much worse."

Her grim humor did not do much to raise the Gunsmith's spirits.

THIRTY-SIX

Maybe it was plain crazy, but they followed Geronimo and his raiding warriors all the rest of that day.
When night came, they camped near him and watched
his fire until they fell into an uneasy sleep. In the morning, they were awakened by the Apache and made to
understand that they would have to be blindfolded.

That was a difficult decision for Clint to make. But
they had long since passed the point of no return. They
were now entirely subject to Geronimo's mercy and
sense of fair trading. So they submitted to the blindfolds
and when they were killed immediately, Clint figured
that they were going to be all right at least until they
reached the lair of this tiger.

The blindfolds were removed at noon. They were in a
long, steep-sided canyon filled with grass, trees and a
stream that bubbled right out of the earth. And just
ahead was Geronimo's camp.

It was a sight bigger than Caddo's but not as big as
you'd expect for someone who held the entire southwest
and northern provinces of Mexico in continual terror.
Clint judged there were about a hundred families and
maybe seventy Apache too old or unhealthy to fight.

But all seventy of them looked meaner than rattle-snakes. Their eyes burned holes through Clint and he vowed that he would finish this trading business and leave within the hour.

"Clint!"

He twisted around in the saddle and saw Juanita Sanchez. She was smaller than he remembered, and much thinner. Dirty, hair tangled, face pinched with hardship and lack of food, nevertheless she was obviously over-joyed to see him. She had been grinding cornmeal with a stone pestle but now she dropped it and came running. An Apache tried to grab and stop her but she antic-ipated his move and ducked under his outstretched arm.

Clint threw himself off Duke and when she hit him running, he hugged her tightly and whirled her around and around for all the Apache camp to see. But this ex-pression of happiness was no act. He remembered this girl, how she'd saved him and made love to him. He ad-mired her, loved her even. He'd set her free if there was any chance at all.

"Clint," she choked, hugging his neck so tightly he thought it would snap. "You come for me and Al-fredo."

"Yes," he told her. "We all have. Will they allow this?"

"I don't know." She pushed back and stared up at Lucy who smiled at her. "I broke my promise to you. I am sorry."

"It no matter now," Juanita said. She turned back to the camp and called, "Alfredo!"

The young Mexican boy stepped away from his friends. He was dressed in only a breechcloth. Clint would not have known him from any of the other boys.

But there was a wide grin on his mouth and, when he came closer, he bowed slightly and stuck out his hand to Clint. "Gunsmeeth?"

"Si."

The boy inhaled deeply and seemed to rise on his toes with pride. "Amigo."

"Si," Clint replied clapping the lad on his thin shoulder. "Mi amigo."

He turned to Geronimo. "My woman and boy. I want to buy now." Clint had thought about this moment for quite some time. He had never bargained with a famous Apache chief before, but he supposed bargaining was bargaining even under the worst of circumstances. You offered little, then went back and forth until you reached some kind of agreement. If they got out of this with any extra money, perhaps Lucy would use it to help Juanita and Alfredo.

Clint gestured to the bulging saddlebags filled with money. "I pay a thousand dollars."

It was a very generous offer and one hell of a lot of money by anyone's definition. The most young and beautiful women slaves were reputed to bring only two or three hundred dollars to the Apache who routinely sold them deep in Mexico. And in all honesty, right now Juanita looked anything but beautiful.

Geronimo considered it a moment, then he made a sharp gesture toward one of his men who strode toward Clint. The Gunsmith stiffened, prepared to draw his gun and at least die fighting. But the Indian wasn't interested in dying. He was interested in those saddlebags. He started to grab them and Chet jumped into his path.

"No!" Lucy cried, as the Apache drew his knife. "Let him have them!"

Chet looked up at her, then reluctantly stepped aside.
The Apache untied the saddlebags and gave them to
Geronimo. He opened one and reached inside to pull
out a thick wad of money. If he was delighted, or surprised or amazed by his good fortune, he did not show
it. Instead, he just looked up at Clint and nodded.
"Your woman."

"And the boy too," Clint demanded.

Geronimo's eyes narrowed and glinted. But he
opened the other saddlebag and his hand wandered
among the greenback dollars. He looked up impassively
but he nodded again. "Your boy."

Juanita hugged Clint again and they grabbed the boy
and threw him up on the saddle behind Chet's horse.
Clint took Juanita and put her in his own saddle. The
poor Mexican girl weighed nothing at all. But she would
fatten and blossom again.

"Thank you," he said to the Apache chief. "We go
now."

Geronimo said, "Good."

Clint could feel the sweat trickling down his spine and
his heart pounded with growing hopefulness. My God,
he thought, we are actually going to pull this off! He did
not give a damn about having to pay the entire five
thousand dollars. It wasn't his money anyway. Just seeing Juanita and that boy and knowing he'd saved them
from years of hardship and degradation made it all
worth while.

He wondered if they wanted to put the blindfolds on
again. Clint hoped not. Smiling, he stuck the toe of his
boot in the stirrup and prepared to swing up behind
Juanita.

"That my woman!" a powerful voice roared.

Lucy gasped. "Caddo!" Her face drained of all

color. Clint swung around and there was Caddo pointing his finger at Lucy. "Me want!" he shouted angrily.

Clint slowly removed his boot from the stirrup. This was going to be rough. They'd already spent all their ransom money on Juanita and little Alfredo. He'd left all their trading goods of any real value in Lordsburg. And they damn sure weren't giving Lucy Covington to the powerful Apache who now demanded her.

Clint's hand eased toward the butt of his gun. If he had to die, so would Caddo and Geronimo. Seventy Apache could not beat his first two bullets.

THIRTY-SEVEN

Chet reached up and took Lucy Covington's hand. "My woman!" he said in a voice that left no doubt he would not give her up.

Clint had already claimed that Juanita was his woman so he sure couldn't pretend that Lucy was his too— Apache knew white men only had one wife. All he could do now was to helplessly watch the outcome.

The outcome was to be decided between the two men. Everyone separated and left an open path between Caddo and Chet. Caddo drew his knife and Chet pulled his own jackknife out of his front pocket and snapped it open. It was a good, functional, everyday knife, the kind a cowboy like Chet would keep sharp and ready to doctor a cow or horse in trouble. But it was no fighting knife and its blade was about three inches shorter than the one in Caddo's fist. To make matters worse, everyone could see that Caddo was much the more powerful of the two men, and a good twenty pounds heavier.

Lucy jumped down from her horse and tried to come between them but Geronimo barked an order and she was pulled aside. Clint looked at Chet and said, "It looks like long odds, but good luck."

"You underestimate me," Chet said. "Just like Lucy

182

always has. There ain't no man with faster hands or quicker reflexes than me. No brag, just fact."

Clint was cheered by those words but he wondered if it was false bravado. "I like your attitude. Just let him come to you. Don't lunge and don't let him catch you off balance so he can gut you."

But it was Caddo who lunged first. He was quick as a cat. When Chet sprang back, the front of his cowboy shirt was ripped and darkening with blood. Lucy bit her knuckles and struggled to free herself.

"Stay put, darlin'," Chet ordered. "I just got scratched a mite."

Caddo lunged again and this time, Chet chopped his left hand down across the man's forearm and blocked the thrust. At the same instant, and so fast that his hand could hardly be seen, Chet stabbed at Caddo. His blade scored across the Apache's shoulder. The tribe displayed as much shock and amazement as Apache were capable of showing. They pressed closer. Some of the warriors began to chant and stomp their feet.

Caddo stared at his bloody shoulder. He seemed more outraged than surprised. He switched his knife to his left hand and began to circle. Chet went right with him. A ballet in death. A thing of stark beauty. Two finely proportioned men fighting to the death.

Chet stabbed out. Caddo parried and their blades locked. Here, Chet was no match and the Apache threw him backward. He struck the ground and rolled as Caddo came down for the kill. They were both on their feet in an instant. The Apache were silent now. They seemed to realize that this contest could go either way. Before it had been sport. Caddo's sport. Not anymore.

Caddo feinted a thrust. For an instant, Chet was deceived and went for it. Caddo's blade whipped out and

sliced at his forearm. Lucy screamed and the sound
drove Caddo in for the finishing thrust of steel. But
Chet was much the taller man, with much the longer
reach. Both their arms sprang to their full lengths, and
despite his shorter blade, Chet's knifeblade sank while
the Apache's came up short. The cowboy's pocket knife
entered the Apache just below the ribs and Caddo stiffened and tried to get his steel into Chet. But he could
not. The Indian's face twisted in a mixture of hatred
and amazement, of agony and horror. He hung between
life and death for a moment and when Chet yanked
his blade free, the Apache plunged into the dirt and
breathed no more.

Chet, bloodstained and now suddenly bent and very
weary looking, beckoned Lucy to his side and said di-
rectly to Geronimo. "My woman!"

Lucy hugged him with fierce pride and love. "Yes,"
she whispered. "Your woman for as long as we live!"

The Apache chief may or may not have understood
her words. But he obviously struggled and the signs of
that inner struggle could be seen in every line of his piti-
less face. This was a matter of honor. He had no choice.
The issue had been decided fairly and he could not kill
the victor.

"Go!" he hissed. "I kill you next."

Chet swallowed and replied, "Not unless you chase us
clear to Wyoming."

So they remounted and rode away without the blindfolds. They did not look back at the Apache or their
hidden valley.

THIRTY-EIGHT

Geronimo let them pass out of the rugged Mogollon Mountains. They entered Lordsburg and left it one day later after buying some fresh horses and supplies. They all felt as though they had been given a reprieve on life. Lucy fussed like a young hen over her rooster around Chet and his knife wounds.

And maybe the cowboy let her fuss a little more than was necessary but Clint enjoyed the show. These two would make a fine pair and though he kept quiet, he thought that their decision to leave this country and start out on their own in Wyoming was a good one.

They rode steadily southwest, down toward Broken Lance. Clint wished he did not have to return to face Angus Covington and the whole mess of fighting between the prospectors and that domineering old rancher. But somehow, he knew that a peace had to be made. In truth, he suspected that Angus Covington would have to give in or someone was going to get killed.

Three weeks to the day they had left Arizona Territory, they crossed back into it and when they rode into Broken Lance, everything had changed. The gold rush was over. And Angus Covington had been shotgunned to death by Earl Sturges. The man had gone crazy and run everyone off the ranch to claim it as his own.

"Why don't you stay here?" Clint said to the rancher's shocked daughter. "You and Juanita and Alfredo just stay in town until I get back and this is finished. It's really between Earl and me anyway. I'm the one he wants."

But Lucy was determined to go. "He killed my father. I'm going."

Chet's attitude was the same. "I hadn't quit the brand yet, so that means Earl killed my boss. I reckon I have an obligation to Lucy's father. I'm coming."

"So am I," Juanita said. "And Alfredo would never leave his amigo to fight alone."

Clint shook his head. There was no sense arguing about this. They had all been through too much together to quarrel now. But he'd be damned if he'd allow Earl Sturges to get wild with a gun and kill one of them either by accident or design.

"All right," he said, "but it's been a long, hard trail and the man we face is a crazed killer. I won't allow any of you to risk your lives. Earl Sturges will kill anyone. Especially you, Lucy. After me, I'll bet you are his number one candidate."

"I'll stay back. But I'm coming," she repeated stubbornly.

They rode out to the Covington Ranch that same day arriving about an hour before sundown. Earl saw them coming and yelled, "That's far enough. All of you! Gunsmith, it's time. Come face me alone!"

Juanita grabbed his arm but Clint smiled. "This has to be done. It will be all right. I promise."

He checked his sixgun and started out across the yard. The day was just starting to cool and shadows were racing off the mountains and leaning out from the house and ranch buildings.

Clint began to sweat. Earl wasn't coming out like he'd promised.

Suddenly, Earl opened fire from the window with a shotgun. Clint was at the outer limits of its range but pieces of shot still dug into his flesh.

He drew his gun and fired but Earl had anticipated that and dropped out of sight. An instant later, he popped up again with another shotgun and fired a withering blast that sent Clint leaping for cover behind a watering trough. The shot sent spray into the air.

"I got three shotguns and I'm loading them all!" Earl shouted. "There ain't no way that you can raise up and put a bullet in me without getting your damned head blown off! Try it, Gunsmith! I dare you!"

Clint crouched behind the water trough. He was in deep trouble. Earl had planned this out so that he could not lose. His gunhand was ruined but, with a shotgun, accuracy did not much count.

"Clint!"

He twisted around to see Chet come sweeping in on his horse. He rode like a Comanche, low and fast. Clint thought the fool was going to charge the ranch house and get himself and his horse blown all to hell. Instead, Chet veered at the last minute and pitched Clint four tightly bound sticks of dynamite. They rolled up beside Clint and he watched Chet go racing back out of the yard to safety.

"Lucy!" Clint shouted. "Do you know what this will do to the place!"

He saw her nod and motion that it was all right.

Clint scratched a match on his thumbnail and touched it to the fuse. It sizzled and burned. He knew that Earl, once he realized what was coming, would race through the house and try to escape through the back door. So Clint waited until the very last second. He had always figured, if they used this dynamite at all, it would be to get them out of a bad fix with the Apache down in Mexico.

Well, he reasoned, surprises were what kept life entirely interesting. When the fuse was only a half-inch long, Clint lobbed it at the ranch window. Earl's shotgun blasted at his exposed arm but the sound of it was obliterated by a tremendous explosion that sent smoke and debris flying into the sky.

Clint ducked his head and waited until everything seemed to have landed. Then, he looked over the water trough at a burning pyre. The house was completely gone and he knew there would not be enough of Earl Sturges around to cover a silver dollar.

The next day they all left that place, none of them ever planning to return. Lucy and Chet would settle in the Wind River country and they'd name their first boy after Clint. And they'd catch a hell of a lot of mustangs too—good ones to be sold to the cavalry and Wyoming cowboys.

Clint, Juanita and little Alfredo were heading for Colorado. Clint knew a fine old Mexican rancher named Rafael Alcala. Rafael had fathered six sons and each one of them were created from the same strong and true mold of their father. They were all plenty bright enough to appreciate an exceptional woman like Juanita Sanchez. It would be damned interesting until Juanita picked her husband. Old Rafael would love having a young boy around like Alfredo to teach the ways of the vaquero and the cowboy. And being a successful cattle rancher, the old man would make sure that the boy and his mother fattened up muy pronto.